# PRAISE FOR *A CURSE OF THORNS*

"I love this book!!!! This is my favorite fairy tale and I love how the author told the story."
- Sarah Doster, Swoon Reads

"This was a very fun read. Belle and Bastian were both very likable, and the plot was interesting and engaging. The writing pulled me along without dragging or being rushed...and I didn't cringe once - definitely a feat...I was also very impressed that you made a heroine that DIDN'T get on my nerves. I found her likable and believable for the most part, and Bastian as well." - Celeste Bridgekeeper, Swoon Reads

"Beautiful retelling of the classic Beauty and the Beast. I like the fact that Belle wasn't a helpless damsel in distress but a smart girl with exceptional skills." - Candy, Swoon Reads

"I loved it! Everything was written so beautifully I just couldn't put it down!!" - Tia8196, Swoon Reads

"A curse of Thorns was an amazing reimagining of Beauty and the Beast where Belle had just as many scars as the Beast and was anything but a damsel in distress...I loved Sophie and I loved the smoldering tension you created between Belle and Bastian. I like that he seemed to admire her from afar but really grew to love her when they began to interact. I think it's realistic considering he knows he must find someone to love him to break the curse. I loved their chemistry - before and after his transformation. Completely swoon worthy!
The Hunger Games meets Beauty and the Beast." - Montrez, Swoon Reads

"This is incredible, and it brought me to tears more than just twice! This story is too perfect to be compared to anything." - A.G. Stone, Swoon Reads

"A CURSE OF THORNS is a great retelling of 'Beauty and the Beast.'...In your retelling, I love your Belle! Not only is she a reader, she is also a hunter who kills to feed her sisters. I love how she's a fighter, strong and protective! It's great to see she and her two sisters love and care for each other. I think it's awesome that she works in a bookstore...It's great to see how Sophie talks to Bastian, saying that he's worthy of love. She's protective of him. He has no one else for so long. He needs someone like her in his life, a mother-figure...I do love the idea that they have saved each other
...It's awesome to see Belle and Bastian fighting together like equals! You have a great ending. Although it's a happy ending, I like how not everything is perfect yet (the kingdom), still a working progress...Your book was such a fun read!" - Chen Yan Chang, Swoon Reads

# A CURSE of THORNS

By: Nicole Mainardi

*This book—the first of many to come—is dedicated to my wonderful and supportive husband Kyle, and my parents Joe and Cathy.*

*You loved me unconditionally and allowed me to dream, and so I did.*

"ONLY TRY TO FIND ME OUT, NO MATTER HOW I MAY
BE DISGUISED, FOR I LOVE YOU DEARLY, AND IN
MAKING ME HAPPY, YOU WILL FIND YOUR OWN
HAPPINESS. BE AS TRUEHEARTED AS YOU ARE
BEAUTIFUL, AND WE SHALL HAVE NOTHING LEFT TO
WISH FOR." - THE PRINCE

~ MADAME DE VILLENEUVE ~
'BEAUTY AND THE BEAST'

# PROLOGUE

## *Tale as Old as Time*

O NCE UPON a time, there lay the small, peaceful kingdom of Briar, tucked away near the far reaches of the French Alps. It was ruled by a gentle hand: the king was a kind man, his wife a stern but generous queen.

They had the fealty of the entire kingdom, but they were missing something very precious: an heir. Long after the queen was believed to have any fruitful years left, she bore a child; a son, who they named Bastian. But the queen had lost too much blood in the birthing and perished no more than a week later.

Bastian was a troubled child from the start: his father was too lost in his grief to pay much heed to him, and the crown's advisors twisted and warped him. By his eighteenth birthday, he was a tyrant and utterly vain. It was then that the king fell ill, and within a month, he too had passed.

The young prince inherited his father's throne and all of Briar, but he was too young and ambitious, and his little kingdom wasn't enough for him. He was thirsty for power, and he was willing to do anything to possess it.

Despite Bastian's protests, his father had never given much thought to a strong military and there were few enlisted men he could call upon to help him in his noble cause. This forced the young king to instate a draft that ordered every able-bodied man in his kingdom to pledge their lives to him in the name of conquest. But, even still, he was not satisfied. He still believed his army too pitiful to take control of the surrounding kingdoms, and to face the even more oppressive Regime that had threatened Briar since before his birth.

Desperate, Bastian ransacked every corner of his castle for an old book his father had once mentioned to him—a book of magic, given to his family by one of the fae. It wasn't long before he stumbled upon a hidden compartment in his father's abandoned desk and found it there. Bound in gold and leather, he could feel the power radiating from it, though the paper was cracking and breaking apart at his touch despite the black magic it held. Reading all through the night, he came upon a spell that would give him infinite power.

But, according to the spell, he needed a witch.

As fate would have it, an old, gaunt woman claiming to have magic appeared on his doorstep the very next night. Relentless rain and thunder pounded the castle stones, and, shivering from the cold, she offered him a simple gold ring. She claimed that, with this ring, he could attain the power he sought. And in return for her offering, she asked only for a place to rest her tired bones until the rain let up.

Bastian saw the witch as hideous and didn't plan to let her inside, but agreed to the terms, insisting that as long as she gave him the ring, he would do as she asked. The old woman spoke in a language Bastian had never heard and handed him the ring. Bastian snatched it from her, and the magic rushed through his veins like lightning. The moment she tried to take a step inside the castle, though, Bastian slammed the door in her face.

What the cruel king didn't realize was that the witch knew he would never hold up his end of the bargain, and so instead of bestowing the ring with power, she'd cursed it.

That night, the witch came to him in his sleep, now transformed into a beautiful sorceress. He startled awake to find her standing at his bedside, blinding his sleep-filled gaze with her haunting beauty. She told him of his curse: that he would turn into a beast when he awoke the next morning, and only when he could find someone to love him of her own free will—and he love her in return—could the curse be broken. He tried to apologize and begged her to take the ring back, promising her riches and a part of his kingdom, but she ignored his offerings and disappeared into the night.

Devastated, Bastian fought to stay awake that night, but when the storm subsided, he could no longer keep the reaching arms of sleep at bay. And when he awoke the next morning and looked at himself in the mirror, he saw that he'd turned into a beast.

Golden-brown fur dusted most of his deeply-scarred face, growing thicker around his head and coating his body, leaving not one inch of skin exposed or unmarred. Even the tortured roar that released from his throat when he caught sight of his distorted face was beast-like. Unable to stand the sight of himself, he smashed every single mirror in his chambers with his sharp claws.

After he'd broken every last reflective surface he could find, his hands coated in his own blood, Bastian ordered his servants, who had gathered outside the closed doors of his chambers that they were all to leave the castle immediately and never return. He only demanded that his governess stay with him; she was never to come inside his room except when he was not in it, and if she were ever to sense him near, she would turn the other way. Despite Bastian's obvious unkindness, the governess had no other family and stayed, as was his command.

But there was more to Bastian's curse that the sorceress had not told him: a spell was cast over Briar so that all that lived there would forget him. He would become a legend, a story, a whisper in the woods—he would disappear like a long-forgotten memory in the minds of his people, and would not return to their memories until the curse had been broken.

Without a leader, the army he'd built quickly dispersed, and the Regime began to sink its claws into Briar. The people of his village quickly forgot about their reclusive king and went about their lives as if he'd never existed. The once-sparse forest around the castle became untamed and grew into a teeming black evergreen that hid the castle from the townspeople. There were whispers that there was dark magic brewing there, but no one dared enter the forest when it became overrun with feral creatures of the Beast's own design.

All that was left of the terrible king was his curse—and the hope that, one day, someone would be brave enough to find the castle and break the spell.

# CHAPTER 1

## A Desolate Place

<u>BELLE</u>

I SHUT my book, breathing in the dust floating up from the pages and placing it back inside the loose floorboard in my room. Dousing the lamp at my bedside, I wished more than anything that I could stay in and read all day. But I had to go out into the Black Forest before the sun rose completely, otherwise I'd miss all the good game and we'd have nothing to eat tonight.

Pulling on my leather jacket, I grabbed my bow and quiver from where they lay against the door to my room and swung them over my shoulder. I grasped the cold metal door handle and pulled, the hinges managing not to creak too loudly as I looked towards my sisters' rooms, hoping they were still asleep.

Our cottage was small for how far it was from town, but the isolation kept us from being too involved in Briar and the Emperor that controlled it. Out here, I was almost able to convince myself that we were our own people, free of the tyranny and corrupt laws of the Regime. It was why I was able to hunt for food out in the treacherous Black Forest behind our cottage, and why I always had to remind my sisters that they must never draw attention to themselves.

Making it soundlessly through the living room, I opened the back door next to the kitchen, its hinges not nearly as quiet. Catching sight of myself on the side of a hanging metal pot as I passed it—one of my mother's— I watched my features cringe as the gray early-morning light glinted off the silver scars that marred my face.

I gritted my teeth, my jaw popping in the reflection. I hated being reminded of them every time I looked into a window, or when I caught myself in a shop mirror out of the corner of my eye. It had happened so long ago, but it hadn't healed properly—would *never* heal properly—and I still hadn't been able to get past the way it disfigured me.

Sighing, I tied my brown hair back and quickly turned away, fingers biting into my palms as I stepped out into the early-morning fog.

~

The outskirts of the Black Forest were completely silent. My breath came out slow, deliberate, appearing in front of me like a ghost in the early-morning cold as I strained to hear the sounds the living forest made. There weren't many animals now, unfortunately. It was the middle of winter, and one of the coldest Februaries that Briar had ever seen. Even wrapped tightly in my warmest gear, I had to stop myself from shaking— to keep from losing focus.

But maybe this winter just felt like the coldest because everyone had less food and less coal. The Regime had significantly cut back on the essentials this year, claiming they were running low on resources. The truth was that they had more resources than they knew what to do with, but they were keeping their citizens under strict provisions in order to maintain control, and it was nearly impossible to stand against them. I wish I could do it, but I had my sisters to think of.

Still, I found my frozen toes curling in frustration.

My sister Emily had begged me not to venture out too far today, but the animals were hiding deeper and deeper into the protection of the forest, and without my kills we'd have nothing to eat for the next week. And I couldn't break my promise to them—to myself—to do everything I could to keep them alive. Our deadbeat father had left us in the middle of the night late last summer, just as the leaves had begun to turn. He hadn't even said goodbye; all he'd left us was a note, saying that he'd make everything right again. We hadn't heard from him since.

I dug my heel into the malleable dirt, trying to concentrate on finding an animal to kill instead of my worthless father, and failing. He'd never touched a hair on our heads, but was a horrible, selfish man, something he'd become even before our mother died birthing Lila, my youngest sister. He'd once been a wealthy merchant, but had squandered all of his—*our*—money away on gambling when his small fleet of ships was lost at sea, carrying the largest shipment of cargo I'd ever seen. He hadn't had a job for years after he'd lost everything, and any work he'd managed to find was lost within a few weeks' time.

Since the moment I'd found that note, I hadn't put much hope in him coming back, and he had yet to prove me wrong. I didn't miss him most of the time, but his absence was hitting us hard. It was deep into the winter of the next year, and we were barely surviving.

The muscles in my legs were screaming at me to move from my crouched stance, and the pants I was wearing, while worn and stretchy, were old and still too tight around my legs in this position for comfort. But they were the only pair I had. The wet ground sifted beneath my thick hide boots as I repositioned, thinking maybe today was a lost cause—when I spotted a large stark-white pheasant land not a hundred feet from my hiding spot.

I shook my head slightly, almost feeling sorry for the poor creature, before quietly pulling my bow back with the arrow already in my grasp. I pressed my cold fingers against my cheek, the feathers of the arrow tickling my skin before I released it.

It stayed true, slicing cleanly through the mist, before burrowing itself into the bird's eye. It fell silently to the ground—one of my best shots to date to be sure. I allowed myself a victorious grin as I stood and walked over to the bird. It was moments like these that I truly loved hunting.

Heart racing, I couldn't help thinking about how nice a hot bath sounded after crouching in the freezing air and wet mud for so long. But a cold one would have to do.

As I was binding its legs, almost giddy thinking about how we could make use of the feathers and the gristle as well as the meat, something rustled in the trees just above where I'd been squatting. I immediately straightened, reaching back and gripping the feathered tip of an arrow.

I stayed absolutely still for a long time, fearing that I'd finally been caught hunting illegally.

Finally, after hearing nothing else, I grabbed up the pheasant and hurried back towards home.

# CHAPTER 2

*A Former Life*

## BELLE

"BELLE!" MR. Alinder called from the back of the book shop.

I smiled; he'd probably been waiting to hear the faint tinkle of the bell above the door. Not many people came in here as it was, but I was the only person to ever come in this early. And the cottage I shared with my sisters was a bit of a walk from town, so he was never sure when to expect me.

He peeked out from behind a precarious stack of books, like a rodent poking its head out of the ground, as I made my way to the back and set my satchel down behind the cash drawer.

"Where have you been?" he asked cautiously.

"Oh, the usual, Mr. Alinder," I said, smiling at his usual appearance of unkempt white hair and askew spectacles. I shrugged off my wool coat, one that had once belonged to my mother, and set it on top of my bag. "Off slaying beasts and saving the world."

Actually, after defeathering the bird I'd killed and stringing it up outside under the overhanging roof, I'd read a couple more chapters of an illegal book called *Pride and Prejudice*. It had only come out a few years ago—Alinder had managed to acquire a copy of it through his back channels—and it had quickly become one of my favorites. Even though I doubted I would never find my own Mr. Darcy, I couldn't help getting lost in the story. It was difficult facing the reality of our situation most of the time, and reading books allowed time for myself—an escape from my fate and the fate of my sisters.

He shook his head at me, but I saw his lips tug up in the corner as he turned back to his work of cataloguing the new arrivals. I smoothed my hands down my faded blue dress and pulled my wet hair into a loose braid that I settled over my shoulder, humming a low tune my mother used to sing to me when I couldn't sleep. Alinder usually didn't mind my humming, but he cleared his throat and pushed his glasses back up his nose, mumbling nonsense to himself.

Alinder was an old man, and the only living person in Briar—except for me—who knew much about books, having owned this bookshop long before I was born. He was a brilliant relic of a man, just like the books hidden in the panels of his office and smuggled in a moldy basement beneath his home. If the Regime ever found out that the shop was hiding pre-Regime volumes, the sentence would be death for the both of us. But it was worth the risk to preserve them. I didn't know of anyone else that had the priceless first editions Alinder did, and neither of us were willing to risk their destruction. They were too important.

Thinking about the stowed books, I smiled again, knowing exactly where each title was hidden. As the only other employee of the shop, Alinder had told me where all the forbidden volumes were, allowing me to borrow them whenever I wanted. Even when I was younger, Alinder had read them to me. So, while my father had been passed out drunk at the local tavern every night, Alinder had tried to distract me with fantastical stories. There'd been tales of myths and legends, princesses and prophecies. Alinder and his books had been more of a father to me than mine ever was.

Shifting my weight, I was met with a loud creak from the floorboards, as if the wood was protesting me. But I wasn't surprised by the sound; the store itself was older than Alinder, as it had belonged to his father, and his father's father—long before the Regime had taken over. The floor was chipped, and had a perpetual layer of dust coating it that never lessened no matter how many times I swept. The two large windows on either side of the door, which had once been a glossy yellow and cut cross-hatched with faded wood, were now Regime regulation and had to be cleaned every couple of days. The bookcases were old and too small, and some looked about to break apart, though the books on them were never more than a few months old.

I thought it was ridiculous that the Regime changed what they deemed appropriate reading material for their citizens as often as they did. It was likely that every person who'd ever bought a book from the bookstore had an illegal text somewhere in their home.

I peeked over my shoulder out of habit, towards the back of the store.

Behind me was a small desk where we held books if anyone were to call for them—which no one ever did—and in the *very* back was the locked and windowless door to Alinder's office. I always glanced back there when I came in, just to make sure that Alinder hadn't left the door open by accident. The Regime soldiers never looked there, but I didn't want to take any chances.

"Belle," he called to me again but from another part of the shop, this time with worry tainting his voice. I closed the cash drawer and left my post to find him looking intently at a shelf near the window.

My eyes roved the shelves, finding him interested in one particular book. "How did this get here?" he demanded shakily.

I came up beside him and, without grabbing the book off the shelf in case someone glanced through the window at the wrong moment, cocked my head to read the title as it scrolled down the crimson spine of the book in gold, cursive lettering: *Book of Fairytales*. I squinted at it, wondering how it could've possibly gotten out here. I didn't even remember it being part of Alinder's personal inventory.

"I don't think this is one of ours," I said slowly, confused as I straightened out my neck. "I'm not sure how it got here."

His hazel eyes were wide as he looked between me and the book. He swallowed thickly and spoke softly, "Do you think this is a Regime ruse?"

My hands gripped the sides of my old blue work dress. "They've never been suspicious before," I reasoned, more to myself than to Alinder. "Maybe we just missed it."

But that was a weak explanation, and we both knew it.

His gaze grew desperate. "Please, take it home with you, Belle. Keep it, burn it, marry it off to one of your sisters. I don't care what you do with it. Just get it out of my shop!"

I took a step back, surprised by his sudden anger. He'd never been so rash with me before, especially over a book. His irises had grown to the brightest shade of gray, and with his hair sticking up, he looked like a madman—but then his passion subsided, and he looked older than ever before, his whole body seeming to cave in on itself.

Without a word, I nodded and took the book off the shelf, being sure to keep the spine out of view. Regime soldiers would be making their rounds soon, and though they were usually routine and involved mainly surface searches, they'd been more thorough lately. I had to hide this as soon as possible, and I headed back towards the cash drawer.

But Alinder's reaction made me wonder how it had gotten there. The best case was that he was getting senile and had put it out there earlier thinking that it was a book about flora or home remedies. The worst case was that the Regime—or someone working for them—knew our secret and was trying to get us caught.

The only thing I *did* know was that we were lucky we found it when we did.

I pulled out the key ring from around my neck where it rested beneath my dress, chose the smallest one, and bent down to unlock a panel hidden underneath the cash drawer. I'd have to stash the book there until seven o'clock, an hour before curfew when all businesses had to close up. I sighed, finding that I was shaking a little from fear of being caught. It was going to be long day.

Just as I stood and placed the key back under my dress where it sat cold against my skin, the front door to the shop slammed open, the bell above the door clanging irritably as two soldiers stepped in. I had to stop myself from shrinking back; their dark figures took up so much of the room.

The Regime uniforms were completely black, from the flat caps on their heads to their glossy combat boots. The only splash of color was emblazoned on their neck in a tattoo the shape of an eye outlined in red. These two were no exception, and my heart dropped a little when I recognized one of them. It wasn't a secret that the men who joined the Regime were no longer men—only mindless soldiers. I'm sure I would've been recruited by the Regime by now with my skill in archery, but women weren't allowed to be soldiers. It was the one thing about them I could appreciate.

"Contraband check!" one of them barked out. He took out a small notebook and pen from his coat pocket, and held it out for Alinder to sign.

Alinder took the pointed pen from the soldier with a trembling hand. Every morning, Alinder had to sign that ridiculous ledger, and every morning I watched the Regime take another piece of his soul. I should've been used to it by now, but I couldn't help the way anger simmered beneath my skin, and I bit the inside of my mouth to keep from saying anything.

Shaking his head, Alinder sighed. "I'm getting too old for this," he said, and pricked his finger with the tip of the pen.

He signed the ledger shakily in his own blood while the second soldier walked around the shop and skimmed the shelves. I'd offered on several occasions for them to use *my* blood to sign the ledger instead, but Alinder insisted his old blood was less important than mine. Of course, that didn't matter when it had to be the shop *owner* that signed the ledger, and not just an employee.

I'd asked once why it had to be in blood, but that had been a mistake. I absentmindedly touched the side of my face where the soldier had struck me.

As we'd never slipped up before, they usually didn't look very hard. But this time, the soldier stopped where the misplaced *Book of Fairytales* had been sitting just moments ago, eyeing it carefully. His gaze flicked towards mine as he caught me watching him, and then shifted to glance over my scars. I turned away, staring blankly at the cash box. I didn't want to; I hated the Regime as much as anybody, maybe more than most in this past year. But I had to think of my sisters, and I couldn't imagine what they would do—how they would survive—if I never came home.

Steeling myself, I looked up as the soldier who'd been inspecting the shelves headed back towards the door and told the other one, "Everything seems to be in order."

At that, the first soldier shut the ledger loudly, placed it back into his coat pocket, and added, "Thank you for your service to the Regime. Enjoy your day."

*Blind obedience*, I couldn't help thinking; that had been much too cheerful a sentiment for such an unfeeling man, but I imagined it had been drilled into their heads since their first day of training. They clicked their heels together once, inclined their heads mechanically towards Alinder, and then left out the front door, ignoring me completely. The bell above the door tinkled softly this time, seeming much happier about their departure.

Alinder let out an audible breath, and I almost laughed—even *I* felt like I hadn't breathed properly since the Regime soldiers had entered the shop. Maybe before that.

"That was close," Alinder muttered. "Too close."

"That's an understatement," I agreed softly, slumping against the leather stool behind me. "I still can't believe you found that book in time. I can't imagine…"

Alinder looked at me over his spectacles, the tiny green flecks in his eyes making it look as if the colors were constantly moving, like a brewing storm. "I've lived my life, Belle. I would gladly forfeit it for yours, should the occasion arise."

"It wo—"

Alinder held up his hand, cutting me off. "But it might. I want you to know that you've been like a daughter to me all these years when I've had no one." He hobbled over to stand in front of the cashbox. His brow was drawn down in sadness. "There's so much goodness in you. Never lose that, Belle. Promise me." Grabbing my hands, he held them in his cold, paper-thin ones. "Promise me that you'll never lose sight of who you are, no matter how hard they try to break you."

I swallowed. I couldn't remember the last time he'd been this serious. "Alinder, I—"

"Please," he pleaded, squeezing my hands tighter. "This place will be yours once I go, and I don't want them to change you like they did me."

"You—you're giving me the shop?" I asked in disbelief—it was the only thing he'd said that I'd managed to process.

A small, sad smile touched his cracked lips. "As I said, you're practically a daughter to me. My own flesh and blood for all intents and purposes," he explained. "And since I have no family to speak of, it seems only right that you should have this place and all its contents when I'm gone. I know you'll take care of my books." His smile faded. "But I mean it, Belle. Having to conform to the Regime…it's one of the hardest things I've had to do, and over the years it's broken down my spirit. But you're still young—you still have so much *fight* left in you—and even though you can't fight back now, your time will come. You can't let them make you forget who you are."

"Not fighting back is hard enough already," I told him, "being surrounded by all these books of mischief and injustice." And I wasn't talking about the Regime volumes out on the shelves.

Alinder lowered his voice. "Words are dangerous, Belle. It's why most pre-Regime books have been banned upon penalty of death." He scoffed. "But you have to give them credit—they didn't burn the books. No, that would've been too obvious. Instead, they simply got people to stop reading them." He gestured around the empty shop. "And look what it's done."

"If anything," I spoke up after a moment, "the ban has only made me want to read *more*."

I'd expected a smile from that, but he just frowned. "You're one of the few crusaders of the written word left." His hands loosened on mine. "All you can do is hope that your small acts of rebellion won't get you and your family in trouble. Don't forget, *I* have very little to lose, Belle."

With that, he patted my hands before letting them go. Heart in my throat, I watched him as he sat down tiredly at his desk and remained unusually quiet for the rest of the day.

~

The hours passed gruelingly slow, and I found myself looking out the window so often that I began to feel a crick in my neck. Alinder noticed my uneasiness and told me to go home. I felt bad for leaving him alone with the shop, especially if the Regime returned, and tried to protest. But he could see that I couldn't stay there any longer, and insisted I take the rest of the day off.

After leaving a distracted Alinder, I headed for the market. I was worried about being caught with the book of fairytales that I'd shoved into the deepest part of my satchel, but I needed to buy bread for the next week and this was the only time I'd be able to do it.

The streets were crowded; despite the bleak weather, most of the vendors were still out and about before curfew. The Regime claimed the curfew was for our own good, but I knew that wasn't true. They only did things for themselves.

Sidestepping a runaway chicken clucking frantically, I fought through the throng of people towards the bakery. Around me, gray tents scattered the streets, bleeding into the dark snow clouds that had settled above us, the street lamps barely giving off enough light to brighten the old cobblestone as I watched someone slip something to a customer and turn away.

The Regime had little restriction on the food they allowed the vendors to sell, but that was where their generosity stopped. If you knew one of the merchants well enough, they might be willing to sell you a bauble or two from the time before the Regime. But it wasn't as common as it used to be. Too many tradesmen had gotten caught by undercover Regime soldiers who'd once been citizens of Briar, and no one was willing to risk death just to make a few more coin.

I overheard the end of what sounded like a heated exchange when I passed by the butcher's, hearing something about "poulet sec" and "boeuf gras" and a handful of obscenities in between. I remembered poulet was chicken and boeuf was beef, but that was about the extent of my knowledge of the French language.

The conversations at the market were strange to me, and hard to follow. Many of the tent-owners were older, like Alinder, and had lived in Briar all their lives. They knew nothing beyond this life—not that I knew much beyond it either—and they still spoke the old tongue.

Briar used to be a small kingdom in a country that had been known as France. When the Regime first took power just under a quarter of a century ago, nearly all of France became part of the Regime. Briar, however, had been allowed by the Emperor to keep their own royalty since we were so small. It was why the Regime hadn't fully claimed it under their rule, and why the elder people of Briar were allowed to speak French out in the open. As far as its citizens were concerned, Briar still belonged to itself—for now.

Sadly, the little bit of culture we had left didn't work in my favor. As French was the language the older people of the town knew best, sometimes that's all they would respond to when talking business. I'd had to learn rudimentary terms in order to get food on the table. I was surprised that the Regime didn't mind the use of the old language, but I supposed they figured that those who knew it would eventually die off without passing it on. Even during my time at school, no other language besides English was allowed to be taught in Regime territories. And it was only a matter time before the French language would be gone completely.

Catching the scent of bread and sugar, I finally reached the bakery on the other side of the square, feeling slightly out of the breath. I glanced up at the sign, the word *boulangerie* scrolled across the wood in large lettering. A part of me hoped it was the son that answered today and not the father, just so that I wouldn't have to stumble through my French. But a bigger part of me wanted the opposite, and a lump formed in my throat as I stepped up under the green awning.

"Bonjour," I called. The baker's son came out from behind one of the large ovens and smiled when he saw me, white smudges marring his cheeks and neck. I forced myself to smile back, feeling my body tense unwittingly.

Sean Ager had been wanting to marry me since the first day we'd met at school when we were eight years old. He'd once been a sweet boy, and his persistence was endearing, but getting to know him over the years had made me realize that he was dull, narrow-minded, and—as Alinder put it—a bit stupid. His only redeeming qualities were that he was easy on the eyes and that he'd been kind to me, for the most part.

I grimaced. I knew it sounded shallow, but there was no one in Briar that I had any interest in marrying, least of all one of the few people who knew my secret. Besides, I had no choice in the matter.

He gave me a dimpled smile, and a piece of his strawberry-blonde hair fell in front of his green eyes. "Bonjour, Belle," he said in reply.

I nodded at him, taking a breath before I spoke again. "Erm, avez-vous du…bon pain—"

"Don't worry, father's not here," he interrupted with a grin, and though I hated the way he always interrupted me, I was glad he stopped me before I made a fool of myself. Sean's father, Aiden, wouldn't even acknowledge me if I didn't speak to him in French, which made buying bread very difficult when he was around. I always seemed to say it wrong, and he'd make me say it again and again until I got it right.

"But you're getting better," he commended, and I felt a bit of heat splash red on my cheeks. "Let me get you a loaf of the brioche."

I nodded, and it was only a moment before he came back with the loaf in hand. I offered him the single Regime coin, the metal warm from grasping it tightly in my fist, but he held out his hand to stop me.

I eyed him suspiciously, my hand falling to my side. "If you don't take it, the Regime will think that you stole from their supplies."

He shook his head. "I've baked all the bread for today, and since I didn't burn a loaf, I had an extra."

Tears suddenly burned in the back of my eyes at his generosity. He had no idea what this meant to me and my sisters. "Are you sure?"

He reached out over the counter and gently took a strand of my hair that had come loose from my braid between his rough fingers. I tried not to pull back at his boldness, my stomach knotting uncomfortably.

"Of course. I'd do anything for you, Belle," he told me. "Maybe if you took your head out of your books once in a while, you'd see that."

My mouth turned sour and I had to bite down hard on my lip to stop myself from yanking out of his grasp. Sean had caught me reading a pre-Regime book when we were fifteen, just before I'd been attacked by a wolf in the Black Forest. I'd been expecting him to tell on me right then, but he kept his mouth shut and helped me hide it in my bag. I thought that would be the end of it, but he knew all too well that I hadn't stopped reading illegal books that day, and he'd always held it against me. I owed him a great debt, but I hated living every day knowing that he could turn me in at any moment if he wanted to.

"There's nothing wrong with reading," I replied automatically.

He gave me a knowing look, keeping my hair in his grasp. "It's just unnecessary for someone in your…situation to educate yourself more than you already have," he explained. "When we're married, you won't be working at Alinder's anymore; you'll be at home, doing the house chores all day and tending to the children." He smiled, as if his words should warm me. "You won't even have time to read anymore."

I felt bile rise in my throat. "Thank you for the bread, Sean," I told him coldly.

His fingers dropped from my hair and he nodded wordlessly. I left his shop quickly and headed home, hating the idea that around this time next year, I'd be married to him, an arrangement my father had come to with Aiden years before I'd had any say in it, in exchange for nearly all the money he'd squandered. Sean wasn't a bad man, but his father had pulled him out of school to apprentice at the boulangerie before he could finish, and now he resented those that were more well-read than him. Which, to be honest, wasn't very much of the population. Alinder and I were greatly in the minority.

The cold wind nipped at my exposed skin as I pushed back through the market, picking up my pace as I ran my fingers in my hair to get the flour out, leaving my hatred behind me. What mattered was that we'd have bread for the next week, and money to spare.

# CHAPTER 3

The Howling of the Wolves

BASTIAN

I KICKED out at the hay-filled dummy chained to the ceiling, taking heed not to rip the material of it with my sharp claws. That would be the third one this week I'd managed to take out of commission, and I imagined Sophie was tired of stitching new ones. But training in my weapons room was the only thing that could take my mind off of my curse, and sometimes I got carried away.

I curled my right fist and my claws dug into my palms. It was becoming harder to keep myself in check these days. Normally, I was very disciplined—I gave myself entirely to the fight, feeling the raw power from my curse flow through me to my limbs and clear my head to focus completely on what was in front of me. Tonight was different from most nights, though, and that fueled my anger.

The blue-fire torches lining the walls flickered as I closed my fist and took a swing, knocking the dummy back only to have it come back towards me again, faceless and mocking. My mind was stuck on her: the forest girl in the hunting gear, who'd taken down a rather large pheasant with a single arrow straight to the eye today. She'd almost caught me this time—her senses were so finely tuned that it was becoming more and more difficult to be near her without her noticing.

The dark magic in my veins took over as I swung again, thinking about the first time I'd seen her. When I felt like I could no longer be at the castle, with its cold walls and stifling stones, I'd dared to travel close to the village. To my Briar.

And that's where I'd first noticed the girl, who had been stalking a deer far too deep into the Black Forest, as I chased the wolves away before they could attack her

Without realizing it at first, I kept venturing out to where I knew she'd be. I'd seen her so often this past year, and I knew I shouldn't be following her the way I was. But, from the first moment I saw her, she'd stolen my breath. She was—

"Bastian," my governess, Sophie, called through the door, and I stopped the swinging of the dummy as her voice echoed loudly around the windowless room. Breathing hard, I realized I'd barely heard her, my mind still reeling from the girl. I took one look back at the dummy, cotton spilling out of the shredded body as if there were a sheep hiding underneath, and growled low in frustration.

I turned back to Sophie, and she was smiling knowingly. "Dinner's ready. You can throw that dummy with the others after."

Smirking at her, I stepped out of the training room and together we walked towards the dining hall.

Sophie peered over at me. "There's something different about you lately. It seems like you've been…distracted."

I shook my head. "I don't know, Soph," I sighed. "I just can't seem to get this girl out of my head."

Panic overtook her features as we entered the dining hall. "You're not going to—"

I tried to keep my sudden anger and self-loathing under control before I answered her. "No. I don't do that anymore. I *won't* do that anymore."

She looked up at me, hopeful but hesitant; I could see that she didn't trust what I said. And to be honest, I wasn't sure I did either.

But the one thing I did know was that I felt lighter than I had in years, and I was certain it was because of the girl with the silver scars.

# CHAPTER 4

*Far Prettier and Cleverer*

<u>BELLE</u>

"YOU CAN'T keep going into the forest alone like that, Belle," Lila told me as she sat cross-legged, her back to the fire. "What if you get lost, or run into the Beast?"

"Come off it, Lila," Emily responded, running her fingers through her wet, tangled hair.

"Why?" Lila demanded stubbornly.

"Because it's a stupid story and completely untrue," Emily scolded our youngest sister, a winter bite in her tone. I'd never told them the story of the Beast because of how relevant it was to us, to how it affected our lives, but I couldn't stop other people from telling it.

Lila's cheeks grew red and she looked away.

"Oh, leave her alone, Em. She's just a child." I stood at our small stove, tending to the tea and wondering what had gotten into Emily. The longer father stayed away, the more the three of us were on edge, but I noticed that Emily in particular had been grouchy lately. "Let her have her stories."

What I didn't say was that, now that father was gone, those stories were one of the few things Lila had left to hold on to. But it didn't need to be said. Father had been gone for over a year now, and the only thing that kept us alive was my job at the bookshop and Emily's work at the dairy after school. It was barely enough to afford coal for the stove and wood for the fire in our meager cottage. The Regime kept all vital resources under their close control, and if you couldn't pay your taxes, they didn't give you another chance to come up with the money. They cut you off for a minimum of three months, and you were lucky if it wasn't during winter. But we always made due.

I also didn't say that I believed the story of the Beast.

"Where do you think—" Lila began after a moment.

"Don't start this again, Lila," I interrupted her softly, setting the hot tea kettle down on a stone pad in the middle of our kitchen table, covering a large crack in the wood. "It doesn't matter now."

Lila nodded smartly and scrambled over to the table, while Emily stood on her bare toes to reach into the single wooden hutch for our old china cups. We'd done the same thing every night now for the past year: the same old chipped cups, the same leaves of chamomile tea that we would use as many times as we could before they were leached of flavor, the same bag of rationed sugar, a small bucket of milk that Emily would bring home at the end of every week—and Lila never ceased to inquire after Papa.

But at least we had bread tonight.

I slathered a bit of the raspberry jam that Lila's teacher had given the class for Christmas and took a bite, my mouth exploding with flavor. I was surprised the preserves had held out for this long.

"So," Emily started as she sat and brought the cup up to her mouth, the steam distorting her features. I sat down beside her with the plate of bread and poured myself some tea, taking a sip as she turned to me. "I heard that Sean is as insistent as ever on marrying you."

I nearly snorted out hot tea through my nose, and it burned. I wondered if this was a new piece of gossip, or if the townspeople really had nothing better to talk about.

"Sean Ager," I shook my head, thinking of our conversation earlier that day. "He's handsome to be sure, but dull and arrogant. I'd spend the rest of my life without any books or stimulating conversation, and half a dozen children nipping at my heels. Yes, I can see it now: my dreams coming true."

Lila giggled, but Emily's face remained stoic, and she lowered her voice as she said, "We'd have more money for rations, and the Regime is more lenient on married couples and their families."

I sobered quickly and sighed. Emily was too smart and too reasonable for her own good. The marrying age was nineteen, and come December I'd be an eligible maiden—that was less than a year away.

"I know, Em," I sighed, "but I'm not quite of age yet. I still have a year of freedom left before I'm forced to marry. I'll not subject myself to something like that until I have no choice."

"But can't you just consider—"

Suddenly, the front door burst open, shattering the brittle wood and cutting off Em's words. The three of us stood quickly in surprise, and I positioned myself in front of my sisters, my heart beating wildly in my chest.

Just under a dozen Regime soldiers in their pitch-black uniforms filed through the door and crowded our living room, followed by the town lawman, Thomas. My stomach tightened at the sight of him; Regime soldiers were one thing—they were a part of everyday life. But if Thomas was here, something awful must've happened.

The Regime had turned Thomas rotten—he was more of a Grim Reaper now than an upholder of the law. The middle-aged haunted shell of a once-good man, he had angry pink scars peeking out from under his stiff collar from a chemical burn he'd gotten as a young man. Since he wasn't a Regime soldier, he didn't have to wear the uniform, and his partially-untucked dark gray tunic and navy-blue pants were both badly wrinkled. I took a shallow, nervous breath and noticed that he reeked of booze. But that wasn't any different from any other encounter I'd had with him.

Every time I saw him, I was reminded that he'd once been in love with my mother, something I'd learned from father one drunken night. But she'd spurned his affections and married papa instead.

I'd seen him at her funeral, inebriated but standing far enough away from the service. When everyone had left and I was having a final word with the groundskeeper to make sure that everything was taken care of, I'd watched him approach her grave and throw himself onto it, sobbing drunkenly. Seeing his body shake with misery, I'd almost felt bad for him then. But he was appointed by the Emperor himself to be the lawman of Briar soon after, and, over time, it had turned him into a monster.

That didn't explain why he was here now, though. I couldn't think of why he might burst into our home with a small army of Regime soldiers like he had, and at such a late hour. Unless something had happened to Alinder—

I heard a muted groan near the door and peeked around the nearest officer to see an older man with them, bound in chains. My jaw clenched.

It wasn't Alinder; it was father.

"Where is Belle Fairfax?" Thomas boomed, breaking through my surprise at father's appearance.

I stepped forward, but still held my arms out, as if they alone could keep my sisters safe from the Regime soldiers. I felt oddly exposed in my winter nightgown, but I obviously hadn't been expecting company, much less Regime lackeys.

"I'm Belle," I said in a smaller voice than I would've liked, but it was all I could manage.

I kept my eyes on Thomas as I spoke, completely ignoring father. I hadn't realized how furious I was at him until just then, but he wasn't my greatest concern at the moment. "What can I do for you gentlemen?"

"Ah, finally, a Fairfax with some decency." Thomas kicked the back of father's legs hard with his muddied riding boots. He fell to his knees in a grunt, the sound of chains clattering to the floor like dropped silverware. I heard Lila make a strangled noise behind me, then Emily shushing her.

"Please," I pleaded. "What is this about?"

Thomas smiled wickedly and stepped further into the room, a Regime soldier following with father in tow. Almost absentmindedly, Thomas plucked up the lifeless, brittle stem of a flower that Lila had picked at the end of summer before setting it back down in the vase, placing something next to it that glinted silver in the firelight.

"I'm so glad you asked."

Stalking back towards father, he grasped the back of his neck tightly, pinching the skin together until it was red; I gritted my teeth. "Your father owes the Regime a great debt. A debt which he's unable to pay." He threw father's head forward with a jolt, his greasy, gray-spackled hair tumbling forward.

Thomas stepped towards me purposefully, but I stood my ground. I would not be intimidated.

"Then, in his desperation," he continued, "he offered up his eldest daughter for the Brothel. As I'm sure you know, employees are few and far between." He paused, and I swallowed the lump in my throat. The Brothel was the worst kind of place, where the seediest of men went to be pleasured by women who were there as punishment by the Regime. My eyes burned at the idea that father had offered me up to work at the Brothel to pay off his debts. It wasn't unexpected after everything he'd done, but it still stung.

"But, seeing as you're Aurora's daughter," he continued, "I've decided to give you a choice."

"And what would that be?" I asked, knowing that it would likely be a choice between the lesser of two evils. And I wasn't sure that the Brothel would be the worst of them.

There was a disgusting glint in his brown eyes when he answered. "It's quite simple, really. Either you come with us to the Brothel, or your father will be put to death."

Lila and Emily gasped behind me. "That's not a choice at all!" Emily cried, but it was Lila this time that shushed her.

I remained silent, trying to rationally consider the choices, and figure a way out of them. If I went with them, there was a chance that father would leave again, and Emily and Lila would be left on their own. If I stayed, father would die because of it. And even though he was a bastard, he was still my father.

Then, an idea came to me—a brilliant, dangerous idea.

Not long ago, I'd overheard a hushed conversation between Alinder and one of the other shopkeepers. They'd been in his office, so I was sure I wasn't meant to hear it, but they'd left the door open and I couldn't help myself.

"Have you heard?" the other man had whispered loudly.

I'd imagined that Alinder had shaken his head. "No, but I'm sure you're going to tell me anyway."

The chair in Alinder's office had creaked before the man spoke again, "The Regime soldiers have been told to be more thorough in their searches. Something about a powerful ring that the Emperor is desperate to get his hands on."

I'd heard Alinder snort out a laugh. "You can't mean like in the legend of the Beast." Silence, and then he whispered, "That's ridiculous! Even if such a thing existed, if the stories are true, he'd have to find the castle and get past the horrible Beast before he could possess it."

"That's just what I've heard, so be on the lookout. I've heard he'll stop at nothing to have it in his custody," the man had concluded before leaving Alinder's office without sparing me a single glance.

The people of Briar were known to gossip about the most foolish, inane things. But the fact that the soldiers' daily searches had seemed to get more thorough after that made me wonder…

"What is it that the emperor wants most?" I asked now.

Thomas looked at me, shock and then suspicion written across his face. "What do you mean?"

I leaned forward. "You know exactly what I mean." Some of the hard glint in his eyes gave way to panic. "Let me enter the Black Forest, find the castle, and bring back the ring the emperor seeks."

Thomas laughed, but didn't skip a beat, and it was then that I knew that Alinder's friend had been right. And that the story of the Beast was true.

"And why would we send *you*, a woman, into the Black Forest? You wouldn't last more than an hour."

"Because I've been there before."

Thomas's eyes widened. "That's not possible."

"Oh, but it is," I assured him, feeling him tugging on my bait. My heart was beating impossibly fast. *This* has *to work*. "I've even seen the castle. It simply depends on how much you're willing to risk." I tried to hide the pleading in my voice, but it was leaking through. "Think of it, Thomas, you'll be the only man in all of the Regime that was able to bring the Emperor the thing he most desires in this world."

I knew greed had gotten the better of him; I could see it in his eyes and the way he puffed out his chest.

"Fine," he growled, conceding. "You have a deal. But if you're gone longer than a month, we'll kill your father anyway." His eyes moved to my sisters and I could feel my nails digging deep into my palms. "And your sisters hold much of your same beauty. I'm sure we could secure one of them your spot at The Brothel. Maybe they'll even take them both." He looked back to me, and I saw his gaze skim over the silver scar that crawled up my face from beneath my nightdress.

My blood boiled, heating my cheeks, but I held my tongue. "I accept your terms," I told him through gritted teeth.

Thomas brightened and clapped his hands once. "Excellent! You leave tonight."

My heart froze and I felt like the air had been knocked out of me. "Tonight! But—"

"Yes, tonight," Thomas interrupted smoothly. "You may have weaseled your way out of my original offer, Ms. Fairfax, but don't think I can't see what you're doing." He waved for his men to leave, and they filed out quickly, uniformly, leaving the door open for the cold to come in and sink into my bones.

Once they were gone, he stepped towards me and said, "You're stalling for time. But I *will* get what I want. And I don't just mean the ring."

Thomas reached towards me, and I stiffened as his rough, unkempt hand brushed my jaw, on the side of my face that was unmarred. Now that he was closer, I could smell the stench on him: like he'd taken a bath in a tub of rum—I could taste it in the back of my throat and it burned.

"You look so much like your mother," he murmured, and I felt like I was going to be sick. But then he straightened, pulling his hand away, his gaze hardening further. "*If* you return from the forest with the ring, you will be my wife."

Swallowing, I looked down at the termite-eaten floor, feeling hot tears well up in my eyes, and then pushing them back to fill the growing emptiness. I'd imagined being married to a man I didn't love, but a man I *couldn't* love? A man who would abuse his power over me? I wondered quickly if my father was worth it. The answer to that was a deafening no. But my sisters were, and as long as they were safe, nothing else mattered. Even being trapped in a treacherous marriage to a delusional psychopath.

"But I'm already promised to someone," I told him quietly, unable to meet his gaze.

He laughed, and my head snapped up. "To who? Sean Ager? I'm sure he won't mind giving you up when it's for the good of the Regime."

*The good of the Regime my ass,* I thought, but I had no choice. Fighting against Thomas would only make things worse. I'd have to figure a way out of the marriage later, when I knew my sisters were safe and cared for.

I lifted my head and answered through my teeth, "Fine, you have a deal."

Thomas, suddenly solemn, answered, "Good." He paused for a moment, looking serious. "My men and I will remain outside until you leave," he said before he bowed his head and left.

As soon as the door slammed shut with a blast of cold winter wind, Lila and Emily ran towards me and wrapped their arms around my waist, the three of us silently crying into each other's hair as I kneeled down. It felt like a hole had torn itself in my stomach—it hurt just to breathe.

"Dammit, Belle!" father boomed, and I started. My sisters took a step back from him, keeping their arms around my waist while I stood again. I'd completely forgotten he was there.

I stared down at him—he was supposed to be one of the reasons I'd agreed to go into the Black Forest and steal the ring from the Beast. Now, I wasn't sure why.

"You were supposed to go with them," he complained.

My stomach dropped, but I ignored it—I shouldn't have expected anything less. I left my sisters' arms and stormed up to father, who was still on his knees and chained by his wrists. He looked so small to me, but as I stood over him, I realized I had no sympathy for him. He'd done this to himself, and now the consequences of his mistakes were bleeding into our lives like mud splattered on a white cloth, and ruining them.

"Oh, was I? And have myself whored out to the entire population of Briar?" I shook my head. "No, I don't think so, father. As usual, I have to clean up your mess."

Turning, I moved to pick up the key Thomas had left on the table by the vase. It was small and silver and icy in my cold, sweating hands. Against every instinct I had, I unlocked father's chains. They clattered to the ground, and he flexed his fingers and rubbed his reddened wrists, looking up accusingly at me as if I'd been the one to put him in the chains.

"I had a plan," he said with little conviction.

Emily snorted and came forward. "Not another one of your hair-brained schemes, father. We've done marvelously well without them these past months."

Father, whose eyes had grown a little clearer, peeked around me at

Emily, and his eyes widened. "Emily," he breathed. "My Em, how you've grown." He grunted as he picked himself up off the ground and approached his daughters. We took a step backward, and he stumbled a bit before righting himself on the back of a chair.

Pain and disappointment crossed his weary features, but it was quickly replaced with resolve. He turned to me. "If you insist on following through with this, then I'll accompany you into the forest and help you find the castle." He looked away into the dying fire, expressionless, emotionless. "It's the least I can do."

Hot rage screamed through my veins at his words. I marched up to him and jabbed my finger into the boniness of his chest; his gaze snapped to mine as he swayed. "You don't deserve to do the least for this family. That's all you've ever done and we're tired of it!"

My voice finished in a scream. Taking a quick breath to calm myself, I began again, more softly this time, "But if I'm going to be away for a while, then I need you here, with Emily and Lila. To care for them as I have." I took a step back, and, seeing father's surprise, continued. "If you dare try and follow me, then when I get back to Briar and marry Thomas, I'll make sure you're disowned from this family in every way possible. I will *not* let you hurt Emily and Lila as you've hurt me." I turned to my sisters. "Girls, come help me pack."

Emily was quick to rush to my room, the same anger and sorrow I felt within myself visible in her brown eyes. Lila, though, stood frozen for a moment, staring at father with her blue eyes—mother's eyes. He wouldn't meet them.

"Lila," I said painfully. Em and I were used to this, but Lila was young enough to still think that father cared.

After another moment of hesitation, she turned and dragged her feet after Em. When I heard the door to my room shut, I approached father.

"I do love you, Papa," I said, and he looked up, hopeful at the sound of my nickname for him from when I was little and mother was still alive. "But if you lay a finger on either of them, or cause them any more harm while I'm gone, I'll kill you myself. Your absence has made me more than capable of taking down an animal."

I turned away from him, not daring look at his expression, to see the look of shock and hurt that I knew—*hoped*—was there.

"They're too important to me—and we've worked too hard—for you to screw things up now."

And, with that, I headed to my room and slammed the door shut.

# CHAPTER 5

The Death You Deserve

## BASTIAN

I COULDN'T believe it was her.

I'd seen many strange things since deciding to take back the only part of my kingdom I dared fight for after being cursed, but the girl never came into the Black Forest at night. She knew the dangers of it, probably better than anyone. Except myself, of course.

Yet, here she was.

I'd been hunting the forest wolves closer than usual to the village when I noticed her at the edge of the Black Forest. Lately, I'd been curious to see what had become of it since I'd become the Beast. Since I'd turned my back on my people. I knew there was an Emperor that desperately wanted my kingdom, but as his own decree dictated, he had to meet with the leader before he took their land so that it appeared more like a peaceful surrendering rather than a hostile takeover. I'd also heard he was getting impatient. But no one dared brave the Black Forest to try to find me and attempt diplomacy.

No one but her.

Her sisters had joined her soon after, the littlest one running towards her and wrapping her arms around the girl's legs, as if she'd never see her again. I hadn't had a chance to see her sisters before, though she sometimes muttered things about them after she'd shot down a pheasant or a deer. They were beautiful too, with no imperfections. But her scar was what had first drawn me to her, and the way the morning sun always reflected off it.

Seeing her now, the jagged silver lines were even more stunning bathed in the moonlight—*she* was more stunning.

Despite the guilt that nagged at me, watching her as often as I had made leaving her more difficult each time: her movements were swift and agile, never ceasing to stun me, but she was gentle with the game she killed. Not a day went by where I didn't watch her.

And without meaning to, I'd found myself falling in love with her.

At least, that's what it felt like to me. I'd only ever felt something akin to love for my parents, and even then, it was for no other reason except that they'd born me. I hadn't even been capable of real love then.

Now, I watched her from my hiding spot, perched in a giant oak tree that I'd climbed up just moments before. She was wearing her dark green hunting pants with a black long-sleeved shirt that clung to her figure, and I watched her embrace her sisters, a few tears fleeing down her cheeks. An unchecked anger rose up in me, and I nearly broke the branch I was holding on to as my grip tightened—the bark of the tree barely breached through my thick skin. I had a sudden urge to approach her and demand who'd hurt her. But I knew she'd run if she saw me. They always did.

Besides, I was too curious.

I focused, slowing my breathing so that I could hear them—to understand what was happening, and why she would risk entering the Black Forest at night.

"Please don't go, Belle," the smallest sister pleaded.

My breath froze. *Belle*. I almost laughed—it fit her more than any other name I could've conjured.

"Why not just let them kill father?" the other sister demanded. Her words surprised me. She had a fierceness in her that was unfounded in other girls her age. That much I remembered, unless things in my kingdom had changed that much.

Then the girl—*Belle*—spoke. "The thought had crossed my mind." It sounded like she was trying to make a joke of it, and my heart contracted oddly.

Her next words, however, came out as a threat: "But he's still our father, and he *will* take care of you. Emily, you know what you have to do. I hate to have to put this burden on you, but… I won't be gone long," she continued. "Before you know it, I'll be back, telling you to make your beds and clean up your rooms." Her voice cracked on the last words, and I felt myself moving forward involuntarily, leaning heavily against the thick trunk.

The youngest sister flung her arms around Belle one last time, latching onto her. The middle sister grabbed her gently by the waist and pried her back, her eyes glassy. Belle's tears had dried now, even as she watched them back away from her.

"I love you," Belle told them. "Never forget that."

The sisters nodded, then fled, away from the forest, back to whatever father they had. Leaving the girl alone.

With me.

She took a stuttering breath and closed her eyes for a moment. It took everything in me not go down there and comfort her. Then she opened them in a snap and, without taking her pack off, ripped a band from her wrist and tied her hair back, exposing her neck. I stopped breathing again as I glimpsed more of the silver scar, the way it dipped beneath her collar and disappeared. Then she moved further into the Black Forest, ever watchful.

I followed behind her, jumping soundlessly between the trees as I tracked her careful movements. I sensed a lone wolf nearby, but it wasn't looking for food. She was safe. For now.

In that moment, watching her navigate the Black Forest at night with nothing but her bow and quiver of arrows, I knew that I would protect Belle at all costs. Even if she would never see me as anything more than a beast.

# CHAPTER 6

*Deep Snow and Bitter Frost*

BELLE

I WAS lying before when I'd told Thomas that I'd seen the castle.

Having barely made it back alive from the Black Forest when I was a child—with an angry but mostly superficial claw mark torn down the left side of my body from a forest wolf—it had traumatized my memory.

When I'd managed to stumble back home, Mother had helped me fix up my wounds before I'd shut myself away in my room and poured over an old pre-Regime map. From what I knew from the story, I'd been close. But I hadn't gotten even a glimpse of stonework. And I'd been lost during the day, when I could see clearly.

Squinting through the dimness of the forest, it was obvious Thomas had expected me not to live through the night by sending me now. But nothing had attacked me.

Yet.

I *did*, however, feel a strange presence following me closely as I navigated, nearly-blind, through the trees. But it didn't seem threatening. It seemed…expectant. Protective.

I shook off the feeling. I was out here on my own, and I had to accept that. I'd taken this responsibility from father and now I had to try to hold up my end of the deal. But it was difficult when I was dooming myself either way—death, or marriage to a man I could never love. Though I preferred the former over death, it was still a hard life to accept.

I shivered suddenly as the temperature dropped, and I pulled my black leather jacket from where I'd tied it around my waist. Emily, with the help of the local seamstress that had once been a family friend before the Regime drafted her son, had made the jacket for me a couple years after mother died. I brought the collar to my nose and nuzzled it; it still smelled like home.

Through my reverie, I was startled by a twig snapping off to my right, and, letting my jacket fall to the ground, I brought my bow up from around my shoulder while reaching into my quiver for an arrow in one fluid motion. But it was so dark—the thick trees kept out most of the moonlight. Fear gripped me and I took an involuntary step back, my ears ringing from the silence, heart pounding loudly in my chest.

I flinched as another twig broke closer behind me, but this time it was followed with a growl. I remembered that growl, would remember it anywhere—the growl of a forest wolf.

I swallowed hard and tried not to make a sound, hoping it would move on. The forest wolves were a hybrid that had been created by the man whose castle I was planning to break into. People in town said that they were part wolf, part Tasmanian devil, but I was fairly certain I'd been the only one to get close enough to make that distinction and be alive to tell it. The forest wolves were vicious and didn't have the capacity for compassion, even for their own kind. It was the reason they didn't travel in packs.

Remembering this, my confidence returned. There was a very good chance that this was a lone wolf. I could handle a lone wolf.

That is, until I heard a second growl, and turned as far as I dared to find another wolf not twenty feet from me, flickering in and out of the soft moonlight that had managed to find its way through the thick canopy.

They were just as I remembered them: jet black fur, red eyes that somehow shone even brighter in the darkness, and teeth the size of my forearm. The one I could see didn't look like it was tensed for an attack, so I risked a glance behind me and found the other one was just as close now. I was thinking of how I could possibly take on two wolves, when, as soon as I moved to turn back towards the other, a third growl joined them.

Heart slamming into my chest, I whipped around to find another black wolf blocking my path. My breath stuttered, clouding up in front of me from the cold—they had me surrounded.

I had a sudden flash of fear for my sisters. Barring how painful death would be, the only thought in my head now was what Thomas would do to them when I failed. And it was no longer an if; I was going to die here, now. But I wouldn't go down without a fight.

I straightened as I watched the first wolf tense on its hind legs, and I pulled back the arrow in my bow just as it pounced. I let the arrow go, hoping the darkness wouldn't inhibit my aim too much, and then ducked forward. The wolf flew over me as I crawled off the ground, the creature landing in a snarling heap against a giant tree trunk before getting back up on its feet swiftly, a broken arrow sticking out of its hind leg. Its eyes glowed brighter as it snarled.

*Great, all I did was irritate it.*

I reached for my quiver to see how many arrows I had left and panicked: only two. In that moment, all three wolves leaned back and bent their front legs, growling with exposed teeth, before they attacked.

And I did the only thing I could think of—I pressed my boot against the trunk of the closest tree for leverage and jumped.

In the air, my hands scrambled in the darkness for something to latch onto, until my forearm thunked hard against a low-hanging tree branch. I latched onto it as I fell, the thick bark digging deep into my skin. I felt blood trickling down my forearm as I hung there, sending the wolves below me into a frenzy.

Groaning at the stinging pain, I reached my other hand up to get a better grip on the wood, lifting myself onto the thicker part of the branch—when a sharpness tore at my leg. I looked down to see that a wolf claw had dug itself deep into my calf, pulling me towards the ground and forcing me to let go.

I screamed, and fell back to the ground hard; the sound of my other leg snapping cracked through the night, and I heard myself cry out again in agony.

I laid there on the dead leaves, the pain forcing my body into shock and freezing up my muscles. I wished I could gag on the smell of my own blood and the hot breath of the wolves as they circled me, but I no longer had the strength. Closing my eyes, I waited for them to tear me apart, the sharp pain now ebbing mutely along my nerves.

*This is it*, I thought. There were so many things I wished I could've said to my sisters, so many things I should've done differently. As I felt the wolves close in on my broken body, their putrid breath filling my nose and mouth, I just hoped against my better judgment that father would take care of them.

But then I heard the wolves whimper, their paws stumbling over each other, until I could no longer hear them at all. My body grew numb from the loss of blood just as something that felt like hands grasped my body and held me in their arms.

That was when the darkness swallowed me whole.

# CHAPTER 7

*More Dead Than Alive*

## BASTIAN

ELLE'S BLOOD coated my fur as I ran back to my castle. I could tell she was losing a lot of it, and quickly—her neck was pushed up against my arm and I felt her pulse slowing. I had to get her to Sophie; she could fix this. She *had* to fix this. My magic could only heal surface wounds, not broken legs. Not gashes so deep that I could see the bone.

I'd gotten there too late. I could tell that she knew I was there; it was the only explanation for why she'd kept looking over her shoulder. So I'd backed off. And the forest wolves, they—they must've been waiting for that, for when I could barely sense her, to make their move. It was what I would've done.

Finally, the castle came into view. The wrought-iron gates opened at my silent command and I rushed through the orange grove, past the tomatoes and squash I'd been growing with my magic during the winter months, and into the castle.

"Sophie!" I boomed, nearly running again as I made my way to the infirmary, the torches on the walls lighting themselves as I thundered past them.

Suddenly, Sophie appeared in front of me in her nightgown and robe, and I almost dropped Belle.

"Bastian, what—?" Then her sleepy gaze settled on the dying girl in my arms and she threw her hands over her mouth. "My stars," she gasped.

"Infirmary," I barked. "Now."

Sophie, who was always stronger than I gave her credit for, straightened. Tying her robe around her waist, she led the rest of the way to the castle's infirmary.

Belle's pulse was a ghost of a thing now—fading fast with each passing moment. I placed her down carefully on one of the cots, watching her chest move slightly and hearing each shallow breath pass her frozen lips as Sophie hurried to get the ointment ready. It was a magic-based concoction I'd created when I'd started hunting out in the Black Forest and had often come back hurt. Almost as hurt as Belle was now, at times.

Seeing her injured like this, I clenched by jaw and my empty hands twisted into fists. She couldn't die—not now. Not when I...

Turning, I punched the stone wall, bits of it plinking to the ground and scattering across the room. I was so angry with myself, I could barely hear anything but the rushing in my ears. If she died because of me—

"Get out of here," I heard Sophie say.

Turning, I looked at her in confusion. There was no way I was leaving Belle alone, not when she could die.

"I don't think she'd want you to see her..." She trailed off, and I realized that Sophie was going to have to cut off her clothes to get to the wounds. "And your brooding is very distracting."

I took one last look at Belle: I didn't want to leave her side, but something told me that she was going to be okay, that Sophie would take care of her—and that if she ever found out I'd seen her without her clothes on, she'd never speak to me.

Without looking at Sophie, I backed out of the room, not taking my eyes off of Belle, even as Sophie began cutting off her bloodied shirt. When I turned the corner, I looked at the wall emptily, listening for a cry of pain or a soft intake of breath at least, but there was only silence.

# CHAPTER 8

*This Vast and Splendid Place*

<u>BELLE</u>

I DREAMT of home in springtime.

The small garden strewn along the edges of our cottage was teeming with ripe vegetables and fragrant herbs, and the grass around it didn't have a single brown patch like it usually did from the Regime rationing the water supply. The corner of our roof that had always been missing large pieces of wood but had gone unfixed over the years looked brand new, and the windows were clean and polished, letting in the golden afternoon light. Even the trees on the edge of the Black Forest looked lighter—as if the dark magic that had turned them had never existed.

But the cottage was empty.

I found myself sitting at the dinner table, clutching a cup of tea that had gone cold. Looking around me, I saw that nothing lined the shelves. There was no rug, no chairs, no mantle over the fireplace. I strained to hear a single sound over the quietness, but there was nothing. Not even the chirping of birds or a slight rustling of the wind through the trees.

"Belle," a soft voice called to me, breaking the silence. I peered into the stifling emptiness, but still there was nothing.

Then, through the open back door, there appeared a woman. She was bathed in a bright, glowing light—it was almost painful to look at her. The loose shift hanging onto her thin frame was a robin-egg blue, tied at the waist with a silver-thread ribbon, and her hair was the golden color of wheat in the summer. Strands of it flew away from her face and caught easily in the sunlight.

As she stepped inside, I noticed that she was barefoot, though it looked like no dirt had ever touched her feet. She was the most beautiful woman I'd ever seen, and something about her reminded me of my mother.

She smiled at me, and the next words she spoke sounded like honey, soft and warm and sweet. "My dearest Beauty, you are too good."

I blinked at her, and opened my mouth to answer. But my jaw wouldn't budge. I tried to make a sound deep in my throat, and still nothing came out.

The woman tilted her head down sadly at me. "I do apologize, lovely, but it's better if you only listen. We don't have much time."

I nodded reluctantly, setting down my cold cup of tea shakily and waiting for her to speak again. Despite not being able to talk, I couldn't remember the last time I'd felt this kind of peace.

"You don't know me, child, but I've been watching over you for a very long time. Your mother was always good to the fair folk, and we haven't forgotten."

*Fair folk?* I thought. *Where have I heard that before?*

Then I remembered reading something about fairies in one of the pre-Regime books I'd come across in Alinder's collection a few years ago. Most of them were just little people who could do small bits of magic, but some were extremely powerful. This woman appeared to be the latter. I wished I could ask her more about who she was, but my jaw remained immovable.

She gracefully sat in the chair opposite mine that had only just appeared, as if out of thin air. The light around her dimmed, and I could see now that her eyes were as green as the spring grass, and her face held no blemishes. She took my hand and warmth flooded me.

"Choosing to go after the cursed ring, to sacrifice your life for your sisters'—it has pleased me greatly. Your mother would've been so proud."

I clenched my jaw to keep the tears away as they burned behind my eyes. This woman—this creature—had known my mother. But how?

"Your sacrifice will not go unrewarded," she tells me further. "Though not many know that magic still exists in this world, you'll find out very soon that it does, and has existed for as long as the world can remember. Unfortunately, I can say no more, and you won't remember any of this until the rightful king has taken back his kingdom once more."

She reached with her other hand to touch mine, softly, as if with a feather. "If the Emperor knew that the fey were still alive in Briar, he'd destroy the entire village and everyone in it."

She squeezed my hand and stood as my head pounded. "Have courage, Belle, and above all, forget not who you are. For you are brave and strong and bright, and despite the fate that's been dealt to you, you haven't forgotten to love those nearest you."

Tears slid down my cheeks at her words, unbidden, but I didn't wipe them away. Instead, the woman reached towards me and touched a part of the scar that marred my cheek; I felt the wet tears stick beneath her fingers.

"Your mother named you Belle for a reason. The world nowadays lacks much salvageable beauty, but one day you'll restore it. You see the splendor in things that have none in others' eyes, though your lot in life has sought to jade you. And that is something to be rewarded."

Her fingers brushed the tops of my eyelids and I felt them flutter closed on their own. "Sleep now child. There is much pain ahead of you, but there is also love."

In the darkness of my mind, I felt her fingers leave my eyes, and I became enveloped in the cold of winter.

~

When I awoke, I was lying flat on something that gave into my weight, and felt a smooth material beneath my fingertips.

My eyes flew open, flitting hurriedly over my surroundings. At first glance, I saw that I was in a very large room that was probably twice the size of our cottage. My vision blurred slightly, and I reached for the leather jacket around my shoulders, but it wasn't there.

*Where are my things?*

It didn't take long to find them. Propped against one of the wooden double doors beside me was my bow and quiver, along with my jacket that I now remembered dropping in the Black Forest, and my pack that didn't look too worse for wear. I sighed in relief.

But my relief left me quickly. Squinting against the sunlight that filtered in through the half-stained-glass window at the head of the bed, leaving warm silhouettes of colored light on the gray-stone floor, I found myself trying to sit up to get a better look at where I was. Without thinking, I propped myself up against the pillows in one quick motion. But my arm screamed in protest as I did, and so I was forced to lay back down.

My heart beat loudly in my chest as I tried to remember how I'd gotten to this strange place—I'd never seen anything like it before. Across from the foot of the bed was a wide set of teal-painted wood drawers, and a space above it that left a shaded imprint, as if a painting or a mirror might've hung there once. Further into the room was a love seat made of purple velvet settled next to a dark-stained wooden coffee table, and beyond that: a large door-less closet filled with fabric and another partially-open door that looked like it led to a bathroom. Porcelain and gold trim gleamed from there in the morning light.

No one in Briar had a home like this, especially with this kind of extravagance. My pulse stuttered as I realized where I was:

Somehow, I'd made it to the Beast's castle.

My gut reaction was panic, and I felt like I couldn't breathe: *How the hell had I even gotten here?* The last thing I remembered was bleeding out on the forest floor, waiting to get torn apart by the wolves. I remembered being lifted up by what had felt like human hands...but then whose had they been when the Beast wasn't supposed to be human at all? Who would be senseless enough to live in the Black Forest?

I looked over at my pack, wondering if everything inside had survived the wolf attack, and whatever had happened afterwards. Using my good arm, I tried to push myself towards where it sat against the door, but I groaned loudly as pain shot through my entire body. I threw the covers off in frustration and, looking down, saw that I was dressed in a black tunic so large that it hung off one shoulder and went past my knees—and nothing else. A strange heated panic rose to my cheeks at the idea of the Beast undressing me, even if it was to save my life.

I took a deep breath to calm myself; that was the least of my worries.

The calf that had gotten shredded by the wolf's claws was bandaged up to my knee, and my arm was wrapped in the same bandages. My other leg—the broken one—was in some sort of splinted cast.

I felt a small pang of appreciation for the Beast.

But, no matter how well I'd been bandaged up, I needed to get out of this bed to see how bad the damage was. I'd thought I was dead, and now I wasn't. And there was no real reason for it.

Ignoring that last thought, I swung my legs off the bed; they felt stiff and ached terribly as I set my feet down on the ornate rug that lay there. I sucked in a quick breath as I put some weight on them and tried to stand. I could hear my heart beating too loudly in my ears again and blood rushed to my head, making me dizzy as the pain spread.

That was why I didn't hear the footsteps swiftly approaching the double doors until the handle began to turn.

Despite the throbbing ache, I lunged for my bow and plucked out an arrow from the quiver. I would *not* be caught defenseless—not if the stories about the king turned out to be true. I pressed myself against the wall, leaning on my one leg as the doors swung open, nearly crushing me. Shakily bringing an arrow back in my bow, I watched as an elderly woman in maid's wear entered. She looked toward the bed, saw I was no longer unconscious in its tangled sheets, and tensed.

I came out from behind the door, having a hard time keeping my shooting elbow up. Or staying on my feet at all. Every movement was draining me, and I found that I was putting too much pressure on the shredded leg. My knees started to buckle.

"Who are you?" I demanded in a strangled voice, and she turned to me quickly, shock written across her dropped jaw and wide eyes.

My whole body trembled with the effort of standing, and I could no longer keep my shooting arm up. I grabbed for the golden filigreed door handle to keep my balance as the world swayed in front of me, and my stomach turned.

Trying to focus on the woman so that I wouldn't pass out, I realized that she was much older than I'd originally thought. Even though she moved towards me with surprising agility, her face was pocked and wrinkled almost beyond recognition, and her hair was stark white beneath her frilly gray cap. Her uniform was a faded canary yellow with white lace adornments that looked like it had been washed far too many times.

She approached me as flitting black shadows swarmed across my vision.

"Oh no, Bastian won't be happy about this," she chided in a raspy-sweet voice, though whether she was talking to herself or to me I couldn't be sure. "Come child, I'll start a warm bath for you. He wants you to look your best for dinner."

I gave her a look that said I thought her mad, but she ignored it and smiled close-lipped—a smile that didn't quite reach her emerald eyes. Grabbing my uninjured arm, she practically carried me with startling strength and cold, bony fingers to what I'd been right to think was the bathroom.

I gawked at it. It was as large as my room back home and much cleaner, the room bathed in white stone and porcelain finishings.

The old woman sat me down on a padded woven stool, but I immediately began to slump to the left as black spots obscured my sight. Without a word, she reached for me, picked me up, and placed me in the bathtub. I tried to feel a sense of propriety when she pulled the tunic up over my head, but I was too drained to feel much of anything besides pain.

Once the tunic was gone, the porcelain tub was flush against my skin—it was freezing, I knew, but my body didn't register the feeling before the hot water from the golden tap began to fill it. Propping both of my legs up outside the tub to keep the bandages from getting wet, she opened a few of the colorful glass bottles placed on a shelf nearby; she poured them gently into the bathwater, and fragrances of lavender and rose and something more pungent filled my senses. She reached behind me to pull my long brown hair from its disheveled braid, and it fell around me in gnarled tangles.

Remembering myself as she reached for my hair with sudsy hands, I told her, "I can do it."

She peered down at me and pursed her lips, but wordlessly handed me the bottle she'd been using. I grasped the green-colored glass with weak fingers and tipped the white translucent liquid into my hands. It pooled easily in my palm, and I sighed from the simple feeling. When I went to reach up to put it in my hair, though, I hissed at the stinging sensation that seared up my bad arm. The old woman wasted no time reaching for the bottle again with an expressionless face, and I reluctantly handed it back to her.

"This will heal you," was all she said, and I realized that she had a strange lilt to her voice. I'd been distracted when we'd first met, unsure if she was there to kill me or not, but now that I had supposed her to be mostly harmless, I could hear that she had an accent that was distinctly French.

It didn't take long for the old woman to wash my hair, and, after I protested again, she allowed me to wash my body with my good arm. I was especially thorough with the places that had been injured, even though it burned something fierce to do so. She left the cast on my broken leg, which was still awkwardly slung over the side of the tub, but unraveled the wrapping around the other so that I could wash that too. I refused to look at it, and it stung like it was being ravaged by a thousand angry wasps when I put it in the soapy water.

After I was through, she held out a white towel for me that looked like it could fit me and my sisters. Sagging onto the stool after she helped me out of the tub, I realized that I did feel better. I shivered slightly, wrapping the luxurious material tightly around myself, and looked at her expectantly.

She bowed in understanding, and I thought I saw a slight smile tug at her lips. "I'll leave the dress that the king expects you to wear to dinner tonight on your bed."

*He* expects *me to wear?* I thought. I tried to stand in protest, but she turned on her heel and shut the bathroom door behind her. Sighing, I dropped back to the stool, and let the towel fall around me so that I could inspect my wounds properly. I turned over my left arm and saw large chunks of skin missing where the bark must've embedded itself when I'd tried to grab onto the tree branch. But the wound already looked like it was at least a week old.

*How long have I been asleep?* I wondered.

I looked down and, unable to get a good look at my leg, searched the bathroom for a mirror. Again, there was none. I awkwardly got to my feet and peered behind me at the back of my leg, seeing that it too looked like it'd had time to heal for more than a few days. I'd have new angry silver scars, but that didn't matter.

I slumped back down and put my head in my hands, threading uneasy fingers through my wet hair. I was exactly where I'd set out to be, but I had no idea how long I'd been here, or how I'd even gotten to the castle in the first place.

The last thing I'd expected to happen was to wake up in the Beast's castle, unharmed, and find myself to be the creature's guest.

# CHAPTER 9

*But in Vain*

## BELLE

IT WASN'T until dusk that the old woman came for me again.

After limping out on one leg of the bathroom, I'd fallen back into the strange bed and sleep had taken me easily for a few hours.

When I startled awake, disoriented again, I was sorer than I'd been after the bath, but not before, so I took that as some kind of victory.

I'd thought about going outside my room, to see what was beyond it, but I realized that, by the time I started to put on the dress I was supposed to wear—which would likely take an eternity on its own—it would be time to meet the Beast.

Now, I stared sightlessly into the empty fireplace, perched on the edge of the extravagant bed. Piled on top of the down mattress were black silk sheets and a thick comforter that I thought was made from the fur of forest wolves. I ran my fingers through it restlessly, dressed in the emerald ball gown that the old woman had left out for me. My bandaged arm looked out of place in such finery.

I hated myself for caving into the Beast's request to wear this ridiculous dress. But what else could I do? I needed to gain the Beast's trust before daring to search for the ring, and if this was the only way, then I had no choice. Maybe he'd trust me enough to wear it around me and I could trick it out of him. Or take it from him, whichever worked.

In my head, I made it sound so easy. But it couldn't be. And I was getting ahead of myself.

If only I had more time to come up with a real plan; I started wringing my hands nervously before I could stop myself and winced at the aching pressure the gesture put on my forearm. A month had seemed so long when Thomas had stipulated it, but now I wasn't so sure.

Finally, there was a knock at the door. At least the old woman had the decency not to come bursting in like she had before.

"Yes," I croaked.

"It's time," she said when she cracked open the double doors, the soft light of the torches in the hall spilling in around her.

I smiled to be polite, but didn't know what to say in reply as I stood awkwardly from the bed. She came to stand beside me and took my arm opposite the broken leg. Leaving the door ajar behind us, I limped as best I could in my matching green slippers into the corridor outside the room. I noticed that, besides the doors that I got a glance of across from mine, here were no other rooms along this hallway, and the faceless walls unnerved me.

It was too quiet.

I was so used to hearing my sisters' constant noise, and the overwhelming sounds of town outside Alinder's shop, that I felt as if the silent stone walls were closing in on me.

Looking down, rich Persian rugs covered the floor, giving the empty, stone-gray walls some color and muffling my footsteps. Swallowing, I focused on Sophie as I avoided looking at the flickering torches, the walls continuing to press in.

The silence between us became awkward as we turned down another, better-lit corridor, and I cleared my throat.

"May I inquire your name?" I asked politely. It seemed only fair that I should know that about her, since she'd seen me completely naked not hours before.

The old woman peered at me in surprise and her steps faltered before she turned forward again. After a moment, she answered me: "My name is Sophia." She looked over, a small smile on her lips. "But you can call me Sophie."

It was a pretty name, but I wondered at the last time she'd actually heard it. It seemed like the Beast wouldn't be one to remember names when he didn't even use his own anymore.

"Is that what *he* calls you?" I asked.

At that, her jaw clenched and her back straightened—I must've struck a chord. I was about to question her further, when the corridor ended and we entered a large room with impossibly high ceilings. Long red velvet drapes were strung up along the rafters, and there was an unreasonably long dinner table that could've fit at least fifty people.

And at that table, a man in a hooded cloak sat with his back to us, most of his figure distorted by a massive, high-backed chair.

"Please," his voice rang out without him turning. He spoke in a deep, imposing rumble. "Sit."

Sophie helped me to the only other chair and table setting, opposite from who I had to assume was the Beast.

I was very aware of how I looked now: the dress he'd given me to wear fit surprisingly well and the skirts rustled around my ankles elegantly. Yet I felt myself sweating. I knew that all I needed to do was get what I came her for and then get out with the least amount of damage I could manage. But all of the stories I'd heard about the Beast suddenly surfaced in my mind, and I found my hands shaking as Sophie lowered me into a red plush high-back chair, much smaller than the one he sat in.

I shot a final glance at Sophie, but she only gave me a small, strained smile and walked back from where we'd come. I stared after her for a moment, willing her to come back, my heart beating hard inside my chest. But when the corridor remained empty, I dropped my head, staring intently at my hands.

*Get ahold of yourself.* Gripping the golden arm rests with both hands to calm my nerves, I ignored the pain in my right arm from the motion, and finally looked up at the Beast.

He was swathed in shadow. His black cloak consumed his entire body, except for a dark pit that the hood created around his face, and his large paw-like hands, which were gloved in black leather. He was so still that I almost wondered if he was real. Then he reached for a glass of amber liquid in front of him, and his hood bobbed forward, keeping his face hidden. I looked at my own glass, willing my hand to steady as I reached for it. The condensation on the outside cooled me when it touched my fingers and palm, but it wasn't enough. I tipped it towards him in silent recognition, then brought it to my lips, taking a long pull of the bitter, stifling liquid so that half of it was gone by the time I set it down again. It burned as it went down my throat and warmed my belly, the sensation a reprieve from the torturous silence.

A low noise that sounded like a laugh came from the Beast. Then he did the same with his glass.

I suddenly wondered if he was the one who'd rescued me from the forest. But that didn't make sense with what I knew about him. He was supposed to be cruel and arrogant and—

My thoughts were broken off when Sophie appeared from a different corridor, but where I might have expected there to be a tray of food in her hands, there was nothing. I looked at her expectantly, then at the Beast, suddenly wondering if he was going to feed me at all, or make me watch him eat and let me starve.

Or...if I was the meal.

"I don't want to frighten you," he began in that same rumbling voice. "Many things about this place *will* frighten you, myself especially. But this castle is filled with magic, most of it my own doing. The kitchen items are..." he paused thoughtfully, "much more vivacious than you would expect normally inanimate objects to be. So, don't be alarmed when you see them move on their own accord."

I narrowed my eyes at him, until I heard a clanging from the doorway Sophie had just come from, and watched a two-tiered tray rolled itself out to us. I couldn't help the surprise on my face; I knew that magic—*black* magic—had changed the king into the Beast, but seeing this magic for myself was another thing entirely.

The tray clattered against the uneven floor and stopped beside me, and I couldn't help flinching away from it. One of the plates, which contained some of the most delicious-looking food I'd ever seen, began to spin itself slowly in a circle and inch forward off the tray and onto the intricate golden placemat. A knife and two forks, one small and one normal, hobbled onto the napkin that had floated up from the bottom tier and placed itself next to the plate. They were followed by another napkin that found its way onto my lap.

When it was finished, the tray zoomed over to the Beast and did the same thing over again. I looked at the Beast—*Bastian*, I remembered—and even though I couldn't see his eyes, I knew he was watching me. But his attention didn't bother me as much as I thought it would, despite feeling completely out of place in his castle.

In fact, if the Beast was always this attentive, tricking him out of his ring might be simpler than I thought.

We ate in silence. Despite my nearly-unbearable need to get back to my sisters as quickly as possible, my last hope firmly in my possession, I couldn't help being curious about the Beast. He may have been a tyrant at one time, but I saw none of that in him now. He'd been nothing but polite to me, and he'd allowed me to eat his food. And if he *had* been the one to save me from those wolves, then I'd completely misjudged him. The story of the Beast that the townspeople of Briar knew seemed to grow farther and farther away from the truth.

The food was delicious, from the arugula salad doused lightly in oil and vinegar to the marinated chick and potatoes. But after my first few bites, it began to churn in my stomach. I couldn't believe I was thinking kindly about the king who'd so easily forgotten about his kingdom and his people. We'd suffered for years because of his vanity, and my sisters and I were in this terrible situation because the Beast had refused to rule.

"You're staring," the Beast's voice boomed and I jerked involuntarily, averting my gaze. I couldn't let my guard down around him, or lose focus.

"What should I call you?" I asked after a moment.

The Beast sat back in his chair, as if he was shocked by my question. "It's been so long since I've had a guest…" he trailed off thoughtfully, then his voice grew hard and brittle. "Beast is adequate."

He pushed his chair back abruptly and stormed towards another part of the castle, his cloak billowing gracefully behind him despite his heavy and purposeful footfalls. I watched him turn a corner, out of sight, and something unfamiliar tugged at my heart.

# CHAPTER 10

## A Great Effort

BASTIAN

REATHING HARD, I slammed the door to my chambers. *Could I have been any more stupid?* What she must think of me now...

I could see her staring at me, like she could see something there, like she *knew* me. And then her gaze hardened and I could imagine where her thoughts had turned to. She'd remembered that I was a monster—one that had abandoned his own people because he was selfish and vain. How could I prove to her that she was wrong when she already thought she knew me? Then again, maybe I was still that man; a beast outside and in—

When I heard a knock at the door, my thoughts broke off, my heart stuttering at the foolish hope that it was Belle. But when I opened the door, it was just Sophie. I should've been disappointed, but I actually felt relieved it wasn't the girl.

My hood had fallen back in my anger and Sophie could see my entire grotesque face, but it didn't matter. She knew what I looked like: a few years ago, she'd needed to tend to me because I was so badly injured from a hunt that it couldn't be avoided. She never brought it up, and I didn't provoke her. It had actually been a weight lifted off me, not needing to hide my appearance from her anymore.

But I didn't want to see her right now, or anyone for that matter.

"What do you want?" I growled.

She stared at me for a moment and my anger grew.

"This one's different," she said finally, and I felt myself deflate, the guilt I carried with me returning with a vengeance.

When I'd first realized that I couldn't reverse the curse with another spell, I'd played within the witch's rules and taken girls near enough to my own age that had wandered too far into the forest to my castle, and tried to make them love me. I hated myself for it, and they'd often ran away in the middle of the night, where the forest consumed them. The third and final girl ran away only a day after I'd taken her—that was when I'd decided that I needed to stop. That I had truly become the beast that the witch had cursed me to be.

That was almost three years ago now. Thought it sickened me to think about it, I was lucky that I'd never actually fallen in love with any of those girls. In a twist of irony, part of the witch's curse stipulated that, if I were to fall in love with a girl and she with me, but then she left me whether by her own will or mine, I'd lose all of the magic I'd come to possess. And with it, my life force—I'd be dead within a day.

I sighed, my anger dropping from my shoulders like a heavy weight, making me feel raw. "It doesn't matter," I said.

I ran my claw-like fingers through the fur atop my head as if it were my golden locks from when I'd still been human. Some habits still hadn't abandoned me, no matter how much I'd changed.

"She can never love me."

Sophie smiled knowingly. "I think you're wrong, Bastian. She came here on her own—for the most part. And you did save her life. I'm sure she's figured that out by now." She placed her small hand on my wide shoulder and looked at me with concern. "You used to have such confidence."

I scoffed. "I was a first-rate bastard, Soph—there's a difference. That witch gave me exactly what I deserved and now I have to live with it." I shook my head. "I don't deserve her, after all that I've done."

She patted my face hard once—she was the only one that could ever get away with that—and pinned me with her gaze. "Don't you *ever* think that you're not good enough for someone. You've more than proved yourself worthy of love, Bastian. Now you just have to show her that you're worthy of *hers*."

I bowed my head and bit the inside of my mouth hard with my sharp fangs until I could taste blood. Having said her piece, she took the hint and left, shutting the door quietly on her way out.

I collapsed onto my bed, staring up at the ceiling. I didn't believe Sophie—not really—but at the same time I couldn't pass up this opportunity. Maybe if I kept my features hidden beneath my hood, Belle would never have to truly see me until she decided that she wanted to.

Until she'd decided that I was more than just a beast, and that she didn't care what I looked like. I would do everything on her terms—I wouldn't even question why she'd ventured into the Black Forest alone in the middle of the night in the first place.

I just had to figure out a way to make her stay.

# CHAPTER 11

*The Boldest Heart*

BELLE

AFTER THE Beast stormed out, I turned to Sophie, bewildered. Her gaze followed him worriedly until he was out of sight.

She turned to me distractedly, "You can retire to your room after you've finished eating, but cannot, under any circumstances, follow me. Bastian's part of the castle is forbidden."

My last bite had turned to ash in my mouth anyway, and as soon as she hurried after him, I bolted up from the table and limped as best as I could back to my room. Once the door was closed, I slumped against it and choked on a sob. All of this at once was overwhelming, and I found it difficult to breathe.

Taking refuge on the bed, traitorous tears spilled down my cheeks and I wiped them away angrily. *I can do this.* As much as he'd hurt his people, as much as I wanted to blame him for my family's misfortune, *I* was the one that had to make it right somehow.

*Make it right...* I thought despairingly. He was a recluse, an absent king, but he wasn't at all like the monster in the story. I remembered again how kind he'd been to me at dinner, how much he'd taken me into consideration. Perhaps he really *had* changed.

Then, an odd thought hit me: maybe I had the chance to do more than just save my sisters.

Was it possible that I could bring Bastian back to life, to make him see that his kingdom needed him? The Regime would have to leave at Bastian's request or risk open war, an act that would tarnish the Emperor's reputation. And...

I wouldn't have to marry Thomas.

It was a petty, selfish thought, but I couldn't help it. With Bastian ruling Briar again, I wouldn't be forced to marry anyone. Not even Sean Ager.

But I didn't know if I could do it. I'd barely spoke a word to him; I hadn't even seen his face yet, and I didn't want to. I was sure he was hideous in some way, but that wasn't it. Once I saw his face—especially his eyes, the windows to his soul—I'd feel like I knew him. I didn't know if I could steal from someone I knew. And, by then, I'd be too far in and there'd be no going back on the plan. Was I strong-willed enough to hurt this stranger, to take his ring from him, no matter the consequences he might suffer because of it, and pretend like I'd never come to his castle at all?

I sat awkwardly in the middle of the extravagant bed, worrying over what to do next. I just kept thinking about my sisters, wondering if they were alright. And father, if he was taking care of them, or if he'd already left them to go on his next bender.

These thoughts filled my head longer than I realized, because, by the time I looked around the room, it was dark. And I was still alone.

~

Later that night, when the far-reaching arms of sleep continued to evade me, there was a knock at my door.

Having finally noticed that the dress I was wearing was digging into my ribs, I'd decided to change into loose pants that didn't tighten around my cast, and a white tunic I'd found in the back of the armoire that was much closer to my size than the black one I'd first woken up in. I'd also started a fire, so at least there was some light and heat in the room.

Keeping the pressure off my broken leg, I peeked out the door, fearing that it would be the Beast, but saw that it was only Sophie. I opened the door fully and invited her in, but she declined.

"I'm simply here to relay a message," she explained, and I plopped back down on the edge of my enormous bed, exhausted but somehow still wide awake. "The king will be gone for a couple days of days, hunting," she continued. "He sends his deepest apologies, but he feels he must get away."

At first, we both remained still, staring at each other, while anger and desperation simmered beneath my skin. I wanted her to tell me *why* the Beast would take a hunting trip at such an odd time. I needed to spend time with him to gain his trust, and I couldn't do that if he was gone.

As if reading my thoughts, Sophie answered, "He wishes to be alone."

I found myself nodding and I turned away, hearing the door click as she closed it behind her.

Anger grew to panic, turning my stomach. How was I going to find the ring now? I had to assume that he kept something so important on his person.

*But if he doesn't,* a part of me thought, *then this will the perfect opportunity to search the castle for it.*

It was a bad idea; I knew it the moment it popped into my head. But I couldn't think of a single reason not to do it. Besides, I had to admit that I was a bit curious. It seemed like this place held its fair share of secrets, and I was sure my sisters would still be safe for a couple of days. At least, I hoped they would. But I couldn't think like that. My father was looking after them, and Thomas wouldn't go back on his deal with me when it was something so important to him. They were fine.

They had to be.

~

I awoke the next morning for the second time not in my own bed.

In my sleep-deprived state—for nightmares of a beast with Thomas' face had plagued me—I couldn't remember how I'd gotten here. But then it all came back to me, like a cold gust of winter wind: my father's return and betrayal, Thomas' ultimatum, the wolf attack in the Black Forest, the Beast.

It was disorienting, recalling all of this at once, and I felt like I might throw up.

I hobbled to the bathroom, still leaning heavily on my unbroken leg though there was less pain in it today, and turned the sink on to splash icy water on my cheeks. I was shaking again and I clenched my fists. Not for the first time, I was glad there were no mirrors; I didn't want to see the lines on my pale face and the worry in my russet eyes. I'm sure I looked worse than usual.

When my stomach had settled, I went back into the bedroom.

My body felt a little better than the night before, but there were still muscles and bones that ached. Part of me wanted to stay in bed, but I didn't have the luxury of wasting such precious time.

I'd slept in my undergarments, so I put on the pants and tunic from the day before and hobbled out into the corridor. There was a tray of food outside my door when I opened it, and the silverware immediately started to clink against itself, as if sensing I was there. It made me smile and I shook my head in disbelief that last night had actually happened, that magic was *real*.

Or, at least it was real here.

I went to reach for a piece of toast, the plate scooting itself closer to my outstretched hand, but my stomach twisted in a way that said it wouldn't like that very much. I gave the tray a forlorn look and continued on.

Low fog made the morning light eerie as it slipped through the slight, high windows. I crossed my arms to keep from shivering in the cold and limped the halls barefoot until I found myself in the same dining room from the night before. The emptiness of it was amplified without the presence of the Beast in it. A place had never felt as hollow to me as this castle did without its master.

I looked around for Sophie, but there was no one. Uncrossing my arms, my heart in my throat, I crept towards the hall towards where the Beast had disappeared the night before, knowing I needed to take advantage of every moment I was alone.

Just as I was about to turn the first corner, Sophie appeared in front of me—I reared back, nearly knocking into the wall, pain shooting up my injured leg. She smiled sweetly, but I could tell she knew where I was going and wasn't going to allow it.

"There you are, dear," she said sweetly. "I noticed your door was open but you weren't there. Are you hungry?"

I was about to ask her how she could've possibly noticed my open door and gotten to this part of the castle before me, but instead I said, "No, I'm not." She looked disappointed for a moment, so I amended, "But perhaps later?"

She brightened before continuing, "Bastian wants me to show you something today in his absence." She held her arm out for me to take, as if we were long-time friends. "Shall we?"

I hesitated only for a moment, reasoning that I could simply come back to this part of the castle later that night, when Sophie was asleep. And a part of me was curious about what the Beast wanted Sophie to show me. Maybe there would be a clue to where the ring was. It was a small hope, but it was all I had. I smiled genuinely at Sophie and hooked my arm with hers. Oddly enough, I felt very comfortable with her. She was my only tie to a world where there was no magic, as she didn't seem to possess any of her own.

We started across the dining room, towards a part of the castle I'd not yet seen, when Sophie stopped.

"Oh, I almost forgot!" Stepping back from me and dropping my arm, she produced a large black silk handkerchief from her apron. "He requested you be blindfolded." She chuckled. "Bastian always did have a flare for the dramatic."

Then she sighed in a way that made me think she was always humoring him, and I realized that she always referred to him by his true name. She was much closer with him than I would've thought.

Sophie held out the handkerchief and I considered my options. I didn't think she was leading me into a trap, but I'd been unusually trusting since waking up here. Maybe it was because I was almost certain that the Beast had saved my life, or because Sophie came off as the sweet yet fierce grandmother I'd never had, but I finally turned around for her to put the blindfold on. What did I have to lose?

Once it was tied securely and all I could see was the blackness of the cloth, she led me carefully down one twisted corridor after another. She was surprisingly quick for her age, but then, I couldn't be sure how old she actually was. There were so many things I wanted to know about her, but felt like it would be rude to ask.

Her footsteps echoed loudly against the stone, and I thought she was going to lead me straight out of the castle when we stopped suddenly. Still sightless, I felt her reach behind me and untie the blindfold. As the fabric slipped from my eyes, I noticed that we weren't in the depths of the castle, but we weren't outside either.

It was a greenhouse.

Looking up, there were only a few clouds in the sky, and the sun filtered cleanly through the emerald glass above me, casting the room in a strange light. I took an involuntary shuffle forward but barely noticed the movement—I'd never been so enchanted before.

Reaching towards the back of the room was a long, thick wooden table lined with so many varieties of potted plants that I couldn't even begin to name them all. And they were moving, all of them. They swayed at separate tempos, as if each one was caught in a different breeze or moving to the rhythm of varying melodies, reaching up for a taste of the sunlight. These plants had no flowers—they were completely devoid of any color except a deep, enchanting shade of evergreen that reminded me of the Black Forest trees near home when the sunlight hit them in the summer.

That was why another color caught my eye so easily, and my gaze found the edges of the greenhouse. Thick brown vines sprang up from they were rooted in the ground, crawling up the wall and along the ceiling until they intertwined with each other to create a sort of canopy. And living on these vines were the most beautiful red roses I'd ever seen.

Despite the town's name of Briar, roses were extremely rare. The Regime didn't allow the planting of flowers, or anything else, for the sake of beauty. I hadn't seen a rose since before mother had died, when father had brought her a wild thorny rose he'd found growing near the edge of the Black Forest. That one had been a light shade of yellow that had bled into deep orange tips. It had lasted a long time sitting on our windowsill.

These ones, though, were red as blood.

I stepped toward the nearest bloom and reached out to it, my fingers seeming to touch soft velvet. Closing my eyes at the sensation, a memory flashed in my mind: my mother, tending to her own flowers in the tiny pots we kept hidden in the backyard, teaching me how to nurture them properly and take care of them. She told me to love them like they were my own little children, so that they could grow big and strong, like me.

A tear slipped down my cheek, and I went to wipe it away—when a thorn on the stem of the rose pricked my finger. I hissed in pain and put my finger in my mouth to ease it, the copper taste of blood on my tongue.

When I could no longer taste the blood, I turned to Sophie and asked, "Is this all yours?"

"Mine?" she laughed. "Oh, heavens no! It's his," she explained, a small smile tugging at her lips, and I blinked in surprise. I hadn't expected someone like the Beast to have the patience, much less the green thumb, to grow anything. Then again, it was obvious that magic was involved.

"The waving of the plants is new," she continued thoughtfully. "I'm sure he thought it might impress you."

I turned to hide my face from her. Why would the Beast want to impress *me*?

"But he's always had a better hand with the roses," she continued, oblivious to my inner turmoil, and spoke wistfully. "This was once his mother's greenhouse, and I imagine he'll want to bring you back here himself once he returns. This place was the only thing that could bring him out of his grief after the curse." She paused. "It means a great deal to him."

I felt a sudden rush of sadness remembering that, in the story, his mother had died giving birth to him. At least I'd known my mother, if only for a short time. *But none of that excuses his tyrannical behavior in the past and his lack of leadership now*, I reminded myself sternly.

It was strange how my opinion of the Beast was changing into something I wasn't sure I understood. The confusion I felt was like a thick fog that refused to leave the confines of my mind.

"Come," she said suddenly, and I turned to look at her again. "You must be hungry by now."

I nodded and realized that I *was* hungry, now that I didn't feel so nervous. My stomach grumbled in agreement.

It seemed to take less time to get back to the dining room, since I wasn't blindfolded. But once we made it to the colder great room, I realized how tired I was. Seeing that my chair was still there from the night before, I went to sit down, my broken leg growing weak beneath me. But Sophie shook her head.

"Come now, child," she said to me, nearly at the entrance to the corridor where I'd seen the dinner tray bustle out of the night before. "There's no need to eat out here in this drafty hall when the king isn't around." Then she winked.

I smiled at her unwittingly and followed her, seeing that I'd been right about it being the way to the kitchen. Once we passed the first entryway to the corridor, there was a swinging wooden door at the end of it—the hinges creaked loudly when Sophie touched it.

When I saw what was inside, though, I stopped in my tracks. I couldn't believe my own eyes, and I blinked a few times as if that would change what I was seeing. It was one thing for a single knife to cut a piece of meat or a couple plates to move themselves onto a table, but it was an entirely different thing to see the kitchenware *creating* the meals on their own. I felt for the wall behind me and leaned back on its warm stones, trying to catch my breath.

Sophie looked over at me, a twinkle in her eye. "Magical, isn't it."

I nodded, speechless as I watched a sharp, glinting kitchen knife thinly slice a zucchini, a ladle stir a gigantic silver pot on the stove, an iron take the wrinkles out of one of the dinner napkins—

"How is this possible?" I wondered aloud, and then looked over at Sophie. "How in the world did the Beast *do* all of this?"

Her face fell. "It came at a high price. At first, once he'd gotten a taste of the magic, he couldn't get enough of it." She slumped onto one of the wooden stools in front of the chopping block, the downward swing of a cleaver only narrowly missing her forearm. "His curse was immediate retribution for what he'd done to that witch, and he knew it. Using the magic book kept him from tearing himself to shreds because of what she'd turned him into; it gave him something to *do*, a skill to hone. He never saw the harm in any of it." She sighed. "But magic—especially black magic—has a price. After enchanting nearly every object in the entire castle, he grew gravely ill. I thought—"

She clenched her jaw, continuing roughly, "When he couldn't use the magic while he was sick, the effect it'd had on him slowly faded and he became well again."

I nodded, wondering how close the Beast had been to dying, when one of the trays rumbled cautiously towards me. Atop it was a white, creamy soup and a fresh bread roll.

"Thank you," I said to it as I took the items from the tray, and immediately felt a bit foolish about thanking a piece of kitchenware, even if it wasn't wholly inanimate. But it made some sort of tittering noise and rushed back towards a short wooden cabinet, like it was flustered by what

I'd said. My stomach grumbled louder this time at the sight and smell of the food, and I ate quickly, the hot soup coating my dry throat. When I was finished, the tray came back for me to put the empty bowl on it, and shot over to the sink with a loud metal rumble.

"They seem to like you," she commented, but didn't sound too pleased about it.

I smiled at her with some effort. It was so much warmer in the kitchen than out in the castle. I knew it was because of the oven, but it was nice to feel like I wasn't in a drafty, almost-empty fortress. With the heat of the fire and the warmth of the soup, I suddenly felt tired. Sophie must've noticed.

"You look exhausted, my dear," she told me, coming to stand next to me and taking my arm in hers again. "Let's get you back to your room. Your body's still healing itself from the wolf attack."

I wondered fleetingly how she knew that it had been a wolf attack that had inflicted these wounds, but then figured the Beast must've told her about it. Which was further proof that the Beast had been the one to save me in the Black Forest. I wondered how frightening he must have been to scare off three forest wolves.

As we left the kitchen, my gaze drifted towards the Beast's corridor, and I decided that I *should* try to rest if I was going to come back later that night to find out if he was keeping the ring there. The greenhouse had been wonderful, and what Sophie had shared with me in the kitchen was something I'd remember for the rest of my life...but I couldn't forget about my sisters. They were counting on me, and letting them down meant a fate worse than death, for all of us.

# CHAPTER 12

## *Of Your Own Accord*

BELLE

SUNLIGHT PIERCED my eyelids, and I sat up hurriedly—before falling back onto the pillows, lightheaded. *Dammit.* I'd missed my opportunity. I'd tried to make myself wake up sometime during the night, but I was more exhausted than I'd thought.

I stretched my legs and sighed at the mid-morning sun coming in through the stained-glass window, sucking in a stuttered breath when I felt the bone-deep ache and stinging pain of my injuries. Hopelessness enveloped me.

*When am I going to heal?* I wondered.

The returning thought of giving up and lying in bed all day was so tempting, but I couldn't. Not with my sisters left in the care of our thoughtless father, who'd sooner sell us all off to the brothel than take any sort of responsibility. Fury raced through my veins like a current, and I knew I needed to get out of bed.

Today was more difficult than yesterday. As I flung the covers off and moved my legs over the side of the bed, touching my toes to the frozen stone floor, the cold was almost a relief from the pain. But the moment I put more pressure on my body, pain shot through me like an electric shock and I gasped.

I wondered if I should take another bath in the healing liquids that Sophie had given me that first day, though they clearly hadn't worked as well as I'd thought.

*Don't give up,* I heard Lila's silly voice, clear and piercing in my mind. There'd been more than a few nights in the past year and a half after father left that had hit me hard. I'd tried to keep it from my sisters, but they were more observant than I gave them credit for. Em would always lecture me about my duties to the family since father wasn't around and I was the oldest, but Lila was the softest of us. When I was upset, she would crawl into my lap, put her arms around my neck, and whisper, "I love you, Belley. Don't give up." And that was all I'd ever needed to pick myself up again.

But Lila wasn't here: I'd left her with our father. I'd needed her then— hell, I needed her *now*—but she needed me more.

Gritting my teeth, I stood in one fluid motion, ignoring the lightheadedness and the ache rattling through my bones. The first step was hard and I had to remind myself to breathe through the sharp pain. The second, though, was easier, and I reached out to steady myself on the doorknob. I was amazed by how much of the discomfort I could bear, but I didn't want to push myself either. The fatigue was already beginning to settle on my body like the thick moisture before a thunderstorm.

*I can do this. I can get myself out of this room and find the Beast's ring.*

Even though I'd missed my first opportunity to find the ring, I still had at least one more night to find my way to the Beast's wing without him being there. The castle was huge; there had to be more places to explore. Mother had always told me that I was too curious for my own good—the thought made me smile and my mind was made up.

I put on my pants and tunic that I'd set at the foot of the bed, careful not to disturb the fraying cast around my leg, and took a step outside my room. I'd almost expected the tray to be there again today, trying to guilt me into eating, but the stone hallway was empty.

Standing there, I felt exposed—the castle was startlingly quiet. Not even the clinking of dishes or Sophie's faint footsteps, just the rasps of my short, labored breaths. But I didn't dare risk going down the Beast's corridor during the day. I just needed to get my bearings.

Across from my room was the other set of wooden double-doors almost identical to the ones I'd stepped out of, and I drifted towards them unthinkingly.

When I reached for the handle, I half-expected the doors to be locked. But they swung open with ease, and I found myself in what I thought was a completely empty room. As I crept inside though, I realized that it wasn't empty. In the middle of the room was what looked like a wide, thin bed flush to the stone floor, and on the walls were all kinds of weaponry. Most of them were foreign to me, and the first one to catch my eye was a long, curved blade with a braided leather hilt. Others I remembered from books I'd read about warfare: battle axes, swords of all lengths, long wooden poles, thick chains with barbed metal balls on the end.

I turned as I made my way further inside, feeling very out of place in this room of massacre, until I saw the bows and arrows hung on the wall next to the doors. My gaze caught on something there: *a crossbow*. Those had been outlawed by the Regime, as were most of the weapons in this room, but I'd never wanted a weapon more than I did a crossbow. I wonder if he would notice it missing…

Had I not been so quiet from contemplating my standing as a would-be thief of the Beast's weapons' collection, I wouldn't have heard Sophie calling my name from far off. I rushed out the door as quickly as I could—closing it softly behind me—and limped quickly towards the dining room.

"Is everything alright?" I breathed once I'd reached the long table, wondering why she'd called for me.

"Ah, there you are," she said, and she looked relieved, though it was likely because she didn't catch me trying to sneak into the Beast's corridor this time. "Where were you?"

I swallowed. Even though I hadn't been doing anything wrong, I still felt like I'd been caught. "Just looking around."

She narrowed her eyes at me. "You remember what I told you about the king's part of the castle, yes?"

I nodded.

"As long as you don't forget," she said sternly, then she brightened. "Well, since you're so curious, would you like to tour a bit more of the castle today?"

I hesitated only for a second. What I *wanted* to do was find the Beast's ring and get the hell out of there, but as that wasn't an option at the moment, I figured a tour of the castle couldn't hurt.

I nodded, and she smiled brightly. "Wonderful! But first, we must eat."

Slumping into my seat at the dining table, I thought about how long I'd been here, ignoring Sophie as she chatted on. I couldn't believe it had already been two days since my coming here—it felt like *weeks*. Or, maybe it had been longer; I still wasn't sure how long I'd been unconscious after the wolf attack.

But my thoughts were quickly interrupted when Sophie took a seat beside me in the Beast's chair. I must've been so lost in my thoughts that I hadn't heard her drag the chair over, though I couldn't see how she'd done it on her own.

"My dear," she began seriously, and I tensed up. When I imagined coming here, I hadn't thought I'd be conversing with anyone but the Beast. And the more time I spent with Sophie, the more awkward I'd begun to feel.

"Bastian told me how he found you," she continued. "Why were you all alone in the Black Forest? Didn't your parents teach you never to enter it, especially at night and unaccompanied?"

I swallowed, now infinitely more uncomfortable than before, but thought it would be worse not to answer her.

"My mother—" I started, but my voice cracked and I had to clear my throat. "My mother is dead, actually. And my father hasn't been around very much."

Sophie put her hand up to her chest, her gray eyes widening in sympathy. "Oh, dear…"

I tried to smile, waving away her concerns. "It's alright. When my mother passed, I knew I had to take care of myself—and my sisters. They needed me." I looked down at my hands folded in my lap. "They still do."

She was silent for a moment, before, "Is that why you've come here?" Sophie asked tentatively. "To save your sisters?"

I nodded, fighting back tears. The unfairness of it all hit me again like a cold gust of wind slamming into my chest, making it hard to breathe.

"Well," Sophie said firmly. Then, she snapped her fingers.

I looked up as a loaded tray bustled out of the kitchen. Once it stopped beside us, I saw that it was eggs, bacon, and potatoes today, with caramelized onions. I ate a couple bites out of courtesy, but then stopped, setting the fork down with a frustrated clang. It hopped away from me and back onto the tray—the poor thing looked like it was quivering, but I ignored it, angry with myself more than anything else.

Sophie had dragged my emotions out of me, and I'd let her. I had to focus on the ring; the more I thought about my situation, the more I was distracted.

Then again, I was sort of out of ideas at the moment. It was difficult trying to understand the Beast himself, much less having any idea of where I could begin to look for the ring. He wouldn't leave it out in the open, or even in a room I could have the chance of finding on my own. No, I'd just have to trust that it was either in the forbidden part of the castle, or with him. I could eliminate one of those tonight.

Ignoring the tittering utensils, I told Sophie, "I'm ready for the tour now."

I must've been lost in my thoughts for a long while before speaking, as Sophie had already finished her plate of food. She smiled at me again as she stood, but I could tell by the sadness in her eyes that it was being forced. I wanted to tell her not to feel sorry for me as I got up from my chair, but I was tired of always having to say it.

Without a word, I followed her out of the dining room and into a nearby corridor.

"You'll have to forgive the mess," she told me as she glanced back, matching her pace to walk beside me. "There haven't been many reasons to clean up this part of the castle since...well, since the curse."

I nodded, feeling as if my head was being controlled like a marionette.

"I understand," I said. "I can't imagine you've had many visitors."

Her shoulders slumped at that, but she remained silent, and I wondered what she wasn't telling me.

Goosebumps popped up on my skin the longer we walked: this part of the castle felt colder than any other I'd been in so far, the natural light fading until all that was left were the low torches, flickering eerily.

I felt like a ghost, wandering the halls of a place long forgotten and left to decay, and I thought about all that I'd seen here. The dining hall had clearly held more people at one time, but was completely deserted. There were no servants bustling around, doing chores. No one giving orders. No children playing in the corridors. It was like a tomb.

I hadn't even thought about the people who'd been forced out by the Beast's vanity, until now. The stories never mentioned if those that had once worked at the castle had gotten jobs in the village, if they'd been able to feed their families. Anger grew inside me at his thoughtlessness, but there was also a feeling in the pit of my stomach that I couldn't quite place.

I shivered as the temperature dropped again, folding my arms around myself. I was about to ask Sophie where we were going until, finally, we came to a door at the end of the hall.

The wood was ornately carved and the door quite large, though the gold trimming around it was beginning to crack in some places. Sophie looked over at me expectantly, so I tried the door and it gave in, creaking with the pressure as stale dust billowed around me.

But it wouldn't open all the way, the door knocking into something heavy. I looked over at the old woman again, now a little frightened by what she was going to show me, but she simply stared at me. Swallowing, I slid in first, Sophie right behind, and we were just able to squeeze into the room.

Before I had a chance to get my bearings in the darkness, the torches inside burst to life on their own, and I gasped.

The frozen chamber was so filled with stuff that there was barely enough room to move. I noted that the rest of the high-backed chairs from the dining room had been pushed into a corner, with heaps of elegant clothes and pre-Regime toys piled on top of them. There were troves of gold and jewels and ornate tapestries, beautiful sculptures and paintings of the old king and queen, and even a bed. I wondered what all of this was doing down here. Why would the Beast want to hide these things away?

"Bastian stowed all this here even before the curse," Sophie explained, and her voice cut through the silence so easily that I flinched. The thought that I'd had of this castle being a tomb was heightened here. I was reminded of the way the Egyptians would bury their dead pharaohs with all of their worldly possessions. My palms were sweaty despite the cold at the possibility of finding a dead body down here.

"It was difficult watching him destroy himself," she continued, "but he wouldn't hear a word of it from me. He was so obsessed with power that it overtook him, and he's hated himself for it every day since becoming cursed."

I finally looked over at Sophie, her gaze glassy but resolute, and I had a hard time grasping on to the sympathy she was looking for.

"Why are you telling me this?" I asked.

"Because you told me that you're here to save your sisters, and, I'm sure, to also right some injustice," she explained, "but they're not the only ones in peril. They're not the only ones being wrongly punished. Bastian—the Beast—is no longer a selfish, vain king. He's just a man who—"

"Then why hasn't he taken back his kingdom?" I interrupted her, tossing aside my fear of the forgotten room. "Why has he left us in the constricting hands of the Regime and its corrupt Emperor?"

Sophie pulled back, clearly shocked at my harsh words. I didn't want to hurt her, but I couldn't stop my anger from rising and spewing out.

"Briar has been struggling—*dying*—since the king became cursed," I continued, hearing my voice echo severely along the corridor behind me. "We've had no one to lead us, no one with the power or authority to stand up to the Emperor. We were defenseless and the Regime took advantage. And where was Bastian? He was here, pouting over being turned into the monster that he'd already proved himself to be, hiding from the world—

from his own people—because his vanity had such a powerful hold on him and he was too weak to stop it." I shook my head and clenched my jaw, trying and failing to rein in my anger. "The Beast has lived in luxury here in this castle, without having the responsibilities of a king that we desperately need." I took a breath and my chest heaved. "I'm sorry, but I don't have very

much sympathy for him."

And with that, I turned and limped back to my prison, leaving Sophie in the tomb of thrown-away treasures and lost souls.

# CHAPTER 13

The Time Was Come

## BASTIAN

THE WOLF'S neck snapped easily in my paws, and I dropped its limp body to the ground, brushing my wild mane out of my eyes.

The silence of the black forest pressed in on me as I wiped blood on the bark of the tree beside me, and then jumped up into its branches. I heard the howl of a far-off wolf pierce the night, but I wasn't going to stick around for it to hunt me down. Leaping from tree to tree, I found that I was quickening my pace towards the castle.

I climbed up to a higher branch and looked up at the crescent moon rising over the tops of the trees, the pale light reflecting off the patches of snow on the ground, making them sparkle like diamonds. Curling my claws into the bark, I could feel myself growing restless, something that rarely happened to me outside the castle.

But I knew why.

Even though I'd left to be away from the girl, I still couldn't get her out of my head, and that was a foreign feeling to me. Only in my wildest dreams had I imagined actually getting to know her. But now, I could see her eating meals with me every night and reading by the fire in the library, her helping me trim the roses that my mother had planted all those years ago.

Which was why I'd had to leave.

I was too close to this—I *wanted* it too much. Something in me felt so sure that she'd be the one to break the curse. But I didn't want to put that burden on her. I knew the townspeople told stories about me, and most of them were likely to be true, so she must know by now that the only way I can become human again is for a girl to fall in love with me by her own free will, and for me to love her in return. So far, I hadn't helped that along by being so abrupt with her, leaving her alone with Sophie. Running away hadn't been the best decision, but, despite the fact that my home was a castle, I often felt constricted within its walls. That day, after storming off, I'd needed to get out.

Now, I was perched in the branches of a tree miles away from the castle. This was one of the few times that I was grateful for the Black Forest; you could go fifty feet from the castle in some parts and not be able to see a single gray stone.

The frozen branches below my feet cracked in response to my movements. It had snowed recently, though not enough to make much of a cushion on the ground. Not that I needed it. But there was something about winter, and the snow in particular, that I loved. It was the worst time to grow anything, though I supposed that was what my magic was for. But it was so easy to make your tracks in the snow, to leave a mark on such a flawless world, only for it to be covered up again.

I thought about my parents, about how Sophie had told me that mother had hated the snow and the cold, but father had loved the sight of it. He'd once said to me that it reminded him of rebirth and change, but also fragility. Snow was pure and innocent, but it could be so easily marred.

Remembering this gave me hope that I'd be able to start over. That I was done leaving my dark mark on the world, and soon the snow would fall again and I'd be able to live my life the way I'd always wanted to. To leave a *different* mark on the world.

I dropped to the ground, grinning foolishly. I needed to get back to the castle.

I needed to see Belle.

# CHAPTER 14

## A Hasty Farewell

BELLE

TIRELESSLY, I laid in my bed, feeling like I could sleep away another day and still be exhausted. But when I closed my eyes, I saw all the things that would happen if I didn't get back to my sisters in time with the ring. And when those thoughts didn't plague me, I imagined the forest wolves tearing me apart.

On top of that, I'd started to feel guilty for what I'd said to Sophie about the Beast. I could tell that she loved him like a son, and my words had hurt her. But they were words that I'd meant. I couldn't ignore that the Beast was to blame for Briar falling helplessly under the power of the Regime, but would I have done any differently? After nearly being torn apart by a forest wolf, I'd hidden myself away for weeks. Even when my mother told me that I'd likely have the silver scars for the rest of my life and that I'd have to face the world again at some point, I didn't want to leave my room.

*We're all a little vain sometimes,* I thought to myself, knowing that the blame couldn't be all his. But I couldn't find it in me to forgive him for it just yet. Not when I hadn't gotten to know him.

A knock sounded at the door and I glared at it, hoping that would make Sophie go away. When I didn't hear another knock, though, I grew suspicious. Climbing out of bed carefully, I opened the door to find that the corridor was empty except for small tray waiting for me, a tea cup and tea pot set on top of the polished silver. The tray's wheel tapped at my foot, and I moved aside so that it could come into the room. The dinnerware was getting more persistent—it was endearing.

Sitting back on my bed, I reached forward and picked up the tea pot by its ornate handle. The white porcelain was painted in blues and golds of soft filigree, with tiny red roses popping up between the baroque designs. It was beautiful. I couldn't imagine the Beast owning something so delicate. Maybe it had been his mother's. My mother had loved tea, and she'd always made her own concoctions that she'd then forced us to drink. But they'd never disappointed us.

Smiling at the memory, I poured the tea into the matching tea cup, hot water and bits of red roses filling it to the brim. I breathed in the steam, and it smelled so much better than the tea we had at home.

As I put the edge of the tea cup to my mouth, I wondered fleetingly if it was poisoned. I hadn't been the nicest to Sophie since coming here, but I didn't think she would be angry enough to try to kill me.

Shrugging, I took a sip—before immediately setting it down with a clatter, my head suddenly light and my stomach twisting oddly. *Damn, she really did poison me.*

But the stomach ache went away almost immediately, and something strange invaded my vision. I gripped the sheets under me to ground myself.

I wasn't in my room anymore, that was for sure; I was in the greenhouse. But it looked different. The green glass was cleaner, and the plants weren't moving. And there was a man there. He looked familiar to me, but I couldn't place him. He was tending to the plants solemnly, snipping off the dead leaves and watering the roots that needed it. It reminded me so much of my mother that I felt like I couldn't breathe watching him. Then, someone else entered through the greenhouse doors: a little boy. Right away, I knew it was Bastian. I'd seen paintings of the cruel king before, and this had to be him.

Little Bastian wrapped his tiny arms around the man's waist, and the man managed a smile, turning away from the plants and removing his gardening gloves so that he could take the little boy into his arms. He giggled as the man held him up in the air.

"My little Bastian," he said, but his voice didn't hold the joy I'd been expecting.

He set Bastian down, and the boy looked up at who had to be the old king. His father.

"Papa, why do you come here all the time? There's so much *dirt.*"

The king's lip trembled, and he kneeled down in front of his son. "Because your mother is here, son. Not in the flesh, but in the roots and stems of her lovelies."

Bastian looked like he was trying to understand, but then he turned and ran off, giggling again. The old king sighed, rubbing at the back of his neck as he stood again. He looked back at the roses, eying them with fruitless hope.

"I'll be back tomorrow, my love," he said quietly into the emptiness. Then he left.

The scene before me shifted, turning my stomach again.

The old king was back, tending to his wife's plants. Bastian was there too, looking every bit like the brooding youth I'd imagined him to be. He sat on top of the table, muddy boots on the bench seat, wrinkled papers in his hands.

"But Markus says that the best thing we can do is strike now, before the Regime has a chance to beat us to it."

The old king shook his head, still not looking at his son. "I'm not going to attack a friendly nation just so the Regime can't have it."

Bastian's eyes flashed, and he jumped down from the table.

"You're going to get us all killed, father. Everyone thinks so." He stomped over to where his father was cupping a rose that had just started to bloom. "The Regime is getting closer and closer to Briar, and all you do all day is sit in this greenhouse, being miserable. Mother is *dead*"—the old king flinched; so did I—"and you're going to lose my kingdom too if you don't do something about this."

The old king turned to his son, rubbing at the purple smudges beneath his eyes as he said, "I won't do it, Bastian My advisors do just that: they *advise* me. It is my choice whether or not to heed their advice, and I am choosing to go against their wishes and avoid an all-out war. Can't you understand what that would mean?"

Bastian sneered. "We'll lose everything if the Regime comes here. They'll kill you once they take over Briar, probably me too. Can't *you* understand what that would mean?"

The old king remained stoic at his son throwing his own words back at him venomously. "This is not up for discussion, Bastian. When you are king, you can do as you wish. But I am still the leader of Briar, and I will not put my people through a war."

"They told me you wouldn't understand," Bastian muttered, then stormed out, the doors quaking as he slammed them shut.

The old king, who had been standing tall, collapsed to the floor, terrible sobs wrenching themselves from his chest. My heart ached for him—he knew his son was being poisoned, was becoming something awful. And yet he did nothing about it.

The image changed once more, the glass taking on a hazy look, the doors pushed wide open. In the threshold was Bastian, dressed in military garb. He looked out into the greenhouse with cold, unfeeling eyes before he bowed his head and left, shutting the doors softly.

When they opened again, the figure who stumbled through them was much larger: the Beast. His hooded cloak still hid his features from me, but I knew it was him. With a large paw, he reached for a trowel that sat on the table, collecting dust. Gripping it in his hand, he crushed the wood of the handle and twisted the metal, roaring as he threw it to the ground. He moved violently towards the roses, falling to his knees in the flowerbeds and yanking at the roots. The plants came out easily and he threw them aside before moving to the next one. I gasped at his anger as he roared again.

When he'd ravaged half the wall of roses, he paused, chest heaving, before falling to the ground in loud, painful sobs, clutching at his heart. I leaned towards him without thinking, my hands clutching at the bed sheets when the vision swayed.

The Bastian I'd seen with his father wouldn't have shed a single tear, much less break down completely. But the Beast—the Beast had been broken. Broken by his past, his present, a hopeless future, and guilt tore at my heart.

Again, the scene changed before me. The roses he'd taken out were still gone, but in their place were smaller rose plants. The Beast tended to them, snipping the dead leaves as his father had.

He turned up towards the sun high in the sky above him, and said so quietly I wasn't sure I'd heard him right, "I miss you. I should've told you that I loved you instead of fighting with you." He looked back down, face still hidden. "I'm sorry father. I'll be a better man, for you. I promise."

Then, just as quickly as the visions had come on, they disappeared, and I was once again seeing my room at the castle.

It was completely dark now. My heart was beating so fast in my chest, I thought it might explode. I looked down at my shaking hands, wondering at what I'd just seen. *At least Sophie didn't poison me*, I thought, but it was of little comfort. I don't know how she'd done it—maybe it was the magic rose petals from the greenhouse that had been in my tea—but now, I didn't know what to think.

I breathed out deeply and sat up, watching as the fireplace lit itself the moment I'd looked at it. What I'd just witnessed didn't change anything,

I decided, and I couldn't waste any more time. Bastian's past—his curse, his suffering—didn't change the fact that I'd made a deal with Thomas. The longer my sisters stayed under Thomas' thumb, the more likely he'd be to break our deal and haul them both off to the Brothel anyway. And father would let them go, likely finding a way to strike a bargain with Thomas that might sound a lot like forfeiting their lives for his.

It was time to find the Beast's ring, and get the hell out of here.

I crawled out of bed, finding that I was a little unsteady, and crept across the cold floor, pressing my ear to the door. Not a sound. Forgoing any shoes to soften my footfalls, I slowly turned the filigreed handle that had become so familiar to me and opened the door to the corridor. The dim torches were still lit there, so I kept close to the wall.

The castle was all the more eerie at night. During the day, there were at least the sounds of the forest floating in through the dusty window panes. Now, it was too quiet—I felt like something might jump out at me at any moment. I was sure there were many things I still didn't know about this place, and I regretted cutting Sophie's tour of the castle so short.

When I got to the dining hall, I quickly crossed the cold stone floor to where I'd tried to go down the other morning, where the Beast had stormed off the night we'd eaten dinner together. That felt like it had happened weeks ago instead of only a few nights—time passed so strangely here.

Crossing the threshold of the Beast's corridor, I was almost expecting Sophie to stop me again. But there was no one there.

No torches lined the walls in this part of the castle and the blackness stretched out before me. I reached out a hand and kept to the wall, the other reaching out blindly in front of me. My pulse quickened at the idea of getting caught, first by Sophie, and second—and undeniably the worse of the two—by the Beast. There was no way of knowing what he might do to me if he found me here. I could practically feel his fury at my invading his privacy.

But I couldn't just wait around to gain the Beast's trust when he'd left almost the exact moment I'd arrived here. He'd given me no other choice.

Finally, my outstretched hand fumbled against something—a door. It was cold and metal beneath my touch, and I tried to ignore my shaking fingers. I felt around for the handle and turned it carefully once I had a firm grip on it. To my surprise, the door swung open without a sound. The torches embedded into the gray stone sputtered to life, and I squinted against the light as I took in the Beast's chambers.

The first thing I noticed was the scent, though it shouldn't have surprised me: muted pine and a deeper musk, like that of an animal, hit my senses.

The room was larger than mine, but much simpler than I imagined, considering who he was—or, at least who he'd been. I wondered if the room I'd been in earlier, with all the cluttered furniture and thrown-away things, had been the Beast's chambers when he'd still been human. Even with all the chaos, it had still felt more regal than this room.

Here, there was no carpet, only stone, and my feet froze from it as I stood in place. The Beast's unassuming bed laid off to the right of the door, and while the wrinkled sheets looked silk, it was the only luxurious thing about it. There was a closed door across from me, and an old wooden desk pushed up against the wall opposite the bed, piled high with crumpled papers and yellowed books. They looked pre-Regime and I stepped towards them.

But before I could reach for one, the painting above them caught my eye. It was one of baby Bastian and his parents—even as an infant, he bore an uncanny resemblance to both his mother and father. The king and queen were both gazing at their son lovingly while Bastian tugged on his father's trimmed russet beard and gripped his mother's dainty outstretched hand, smiling.

Something pulled at me heart as I realized that this must've been painted just before the queen died, but the painter understandably hadn't captured her as sickly as she'd been in real life. Tears stung like needles behind my eyes and my throat closed as I stared at them. God, the loneliness; the utter *loneliness* Bastian must've endured, not just from losing his mother before even getting to know her, but a father that had been lost that day as well.

I thought about how distracted the king had been in the visions I'd just seen, and I knew that the cruel king had not been shaped at all by his father, but instead by the so-called advisors that had never had the kingdom's best interest at heart. Cruel men who had only wanted the power for themselves, and had been willing to corrupt a young prince to do it.

I touched the face of the young Bastian, biting my lip to abate the ache I felt for the Beast—when I heard a low growl.

I spun around, my hand still poised as if it were going to touch the painted version of Bastian, and faced what that child had become: the Beast, in full form.

His normally slumped shoulders were slung back so that he was at his true height, and his sharp fangs were bared, blue eyes ablaze with rage. I saw that he didn't have his hood covering him up this time and his entire face was exposed to me. Heart in my throat, my stomach dropped and my limbs trembled uncontrollably. In my foulest nightmares, I could've never imagined anything like this.

Thick scars, both silver and pink, marred his face and neck, and what wasn't scarred was grown over with thick fur: a dark blond color, matted with sweat and what looked like blood. His long, sharp teeth were bared at me, and the nostrils of his small snout-like nose were flared in anger—he reminded me of the forest wolves. I took a step back and my spine hit the desk.

Trapped.

*Stupid, stupid Belle; how could you have been senseless enough to come here?*

"Leave," he breathed out in barely-contained rage.

I told my muscles to move, but terror had gripped me, and they wouldn't obey. Even my lungs had frozen up.

"NOW!" he growled, taking a large step towards me—and I remembered that I had legs. I pushed myself off the desk and hurried past him out the door as best as my broken leg would allow. I didn't stop at the hallway that led to my room, moving past the dining table and down another corridor that was lit but unfamiliar.

My leg moaned in pain, but I pushed myself to go faster as I realized something: *I can't do this anymore.* I had to find a way out.

Not only had I just broken any trust that I may've built up with the Beast, but I'd been blind to how much danger I'd been in by staying here.

All this time, I'd been risking my life just *thinking* that I could get the ring from him. I'd been one swipe of his claws away from being gutted just now.

I couldn't believe I'd thought that I could appeal to his human side— there was none of it left. What I'd just seen had been only the Beast, and I'd angered it.

My heart threatened to pound out of my chest as I hurried recklessly through the deserted castle. Every corner I turned brought me to another stretch of corridor that I didn't recognize, with no doors to hide behind. I began to sob at the endlessness of it. What if I never got out of here? What if the Beast caught up with me? My sisters would never know what had become of me, thinking I had abandoned them as they were carted off to the brothel.

Tears entirely obscured my vision now, and my bare feet tripped on a loose stone. I pitched forward, scraping my hands and knees as I landed hard on them, pain shooting up my leg. I thought about getting up, but I didn't have the strength, knowing that no amount of running would keep the Beast from catching up with me.

Then the sobs released.

I pulled myself up against the wall, tucking my knees up to my forehead, and cried like I never had in my entire life. Emily had always called me the bravest one of the three of us, the one that never cried and never backed down from a challenge. This place had changed me, but I couldn't remember when it had happened. Or maybe I'd always been like this.

A coward. A thief. A failure.

After some time, when my eyes finally dried but were puffy and strained in their sockets, I heard quickened footsteps. I braced myself to get up and run, but my hands were still bloody and they slipped on the stone, stinging like the weight of a thousand barbs. I accepted my fate, disgusted with myself by the surrender, but knowing I couldn't outrun what I'd done.

When I looked up, though, I saw that it was Sophie, not the Beast.

*Not the Beast.*

I nearly choked on another sob as I looked up at her.

"Oh, my dear," she said, her eyes flitting over me, landing first on my puffy eyes and tear-stained face, and then my bloody hands. She sighed. "Let's get you fixed up."

She picked me up from the floor with that great strength of hers and supported a good amount of my weight as we made our way back up the corridor. I shouldn't have let her help me; I knew she was loyal to the Beast. She could be bringing me to him right now so that he could kill me, like I knew he wanted to.

But my hands stung from the scrapes, and there was no way I could make it in the Black Forest with injured hands. The wolves would smell the blood on me before the castle was even out of sight. My only choice was to stay with Sophie. With the Beast.

We passed back through the dining hall and I accepted my fate, hoping only that it would be a swift death. I felt sick to my stomach with the thought of dying. Not because I'd no longer be alive—no matter how painful it would be for me when the Beast ripped me apart—but that my sisters would face a fate far worse than death.

But the old woman took me down a different corridor and I found myself in a room situated much like mine, except that it looked like someone actually lived there.

Sophie's room, I thought.

"Sit," she ordered, pointing at a blue velvet chair, and I did as she said. I closed my eyes as a wave of nausea hit, and felt a wet cloth being pressed against my forehead. "Hold out your hands; this will sting."

She used another cloth to smooth something onto my palms, and it took a moment for the pain to set in. It was only a warming sensation at first, but then I cried out as it sank into my skin. She shushed me—I bit the inside of my mouth to divert the pain. After, she pressed a cooling salve on them and I breathed out in relief, though the pain didn't feel much different than it had when I'd injured them. As she began wrapping them in gauze, I finally opened my eyes and saw that chunks of skin were missing from my hands. But at least the bleeding had stopped.

I looked up at Sophie, her face pinched in concentration. She was braver than I, and much more forgiving, and I couldn't help admiring her for it.

"Thank you," I whispered.

She snorted. "That was stupid, my dear. I told you not to go down that corridor."

"I didn't know—I thought he was gone—I—" I took a shaky breath and mumbled, "I'm sorry."

She looked up at me and I noticed that she was done wrapping my hands in the gauze. "It's not me you should be apologizing to. He has a temper, I'll give you that, but he's had a hard life and he deserves as much privacy as you or I."

Her gaze turned fiery and her nostrils flared. "Just because he's a beast, doesn't mean that he has a heart that can't be broken."

# CHAPTER 15

*Straight to Her Heart*

<u>BELLE</u>

I DIDN'T realize that Sophie had brought me back to my room and put me into bed until I woke to a knock on my door.

My eyes felt like they'd crusted shut, probably from crying. But I managed to open them and squint against the morning light. Out of habit, I went to remove the covers from my body to get the door, but pain shot up from my hands and I hissed.

The events from the night before came rushing back, and embarrassment colored my cheeks. I'd almost forgotten what had happened—what I'd done.

"Come in," I said finally, giving up on moving at all.

Sophie came in, as I'd expected. "He wants to see you," she told me.

Her eyes looked different and I realized they were narrowed slightly.

She was still angry for what had happened. I couldn't say I blamed her.

I nodded and went to work trying to get the sheets off of me again. Sophie watched me for a moment with flinty eyes before a grin crept onto her face and she snorted out a laugh. She walked over to my side of the bed, pulled back the covers, and helped me slide out.

"Honestly, what are we going to do with you?" she asked, looking me over.

*Isn't* that *the question of the century*, I thought.

She helped me with removing the clothes that I hadn't thought to change out of, and dressed me in a long black skirt and thick gray sweater. My nerves jumped up ten notches as she finished brushing my hair—a gesture I appreciated more than she knew—and I realized that I was getting dressed to meet the Beast. Where he might hurt me, or try to kill me.

As if sensing my panic, Sophie stopped brushing and leaned down in front of where I sat on the bed so that we were eye level.

"He's sorry, you know," she told me, and my eyes widened in surprise. But before I could speak, she continued, "He knows he overreacted…but you know that you shouldn't have been there in the first place. He's not the only one to blame for what happened." She looked down at my hands as she said the last part.

I swallowed and nodded, words eluding me. She was right; I'd have to apologize a thousand times over to get back an ounce of the trust that I'd lost last night. And the thing was, I wanted it: his trust. Something from the visions I'd seen last night had convinced me that there was more to him than just being a heartless king that had been cursed to be as hideous outside as he had been inside, and I wanted to know it. Despite what I'd said to Sophie in the storage room, I *was* beginning to feel sympathy for the Beast.

It seemed that the old woman had convinced me after all.

"Alright," I said. "Take me to him. It can't be as bad as last night, right?"

She cracked a smile that brought out her wrinkles and finally lit up her eyes. I wanted to tell her that she needed to smile like that more, but I bit my tongue.

Sophie took my arm, leading me past the tray that waited patiently at my door with breakfast, and could swear the silverware was watching me go forlornly. We passed through the dining hall again and entered the corridor that I'd gone down last night in my haste to escape the Beast's wrath.

"This is the way to the greenhouse, you know," she told me over her shoulder. "You would've made it there if you'd just gone around one more corner."

I laughed. "Of course."

We made it there much quicker than I expected, and without another word spoken until we stopped before the open doors. As I stood at the stone threshold, Sophie beside me, I could almost feel the magic in the plants and blood-red roses springing from the green-tinged sun. But I stopped when I saw the Beast's back facing us, his paws poised tightly behind him. His hood was back up over his head, and it made him seem more like a dark, ominous shadow than a living thing.

I knew he had to have heard us coming, but he still didn't turn. I took an unintentional step away, when I felt Sophie's hand on my back guiding me forward, as if to tell me, "Don't be afraid." But I *was* afraid. I was terrified.

She cut half the space between the Beast and I by dropping my arm and pushing one of her strong hands into the small of my back. Stumbling forward, I turned to her in panic as she smiled encouragingly, then walked out of the greenhouse without looking back. I watched the empty hallway for a moment, willing her to reappear.

But then the Beast cleared his throat.

I twisted towards him reluctantly and was met with the blackness of where his face should've been. He was hiding from me again, and a sudden flash of his true form from the night before appeared in my mind, making me swallow hard. He shifted uncomfortably.

"Belle, I—" he began, his voice soft and low and full of regret. I liked the way my name sounded when he said it...but I immediately shoved that thought away, wondering how he knew it in the first place since I'd never properly introduced myself to him. His chest moved as he took a deep breath, and I watched as he flexed and released his gloved fists. "I'm sorry about last night. I didn't mean—"

"Yes, you did," I said in a small voice. I looked away, because even though I couldn't see his eyes, I could imagine that he was looking at me. "It was my fault. I shouldn't have gone into your room without your permission. It was insensitive of me, and I'm sorry." I walked away from him and further into the greenhouse, hating myself for not being able to face him as I said these next words. It wasn't because they were a lie—it was that they were the truth, and that frightened me. "But I thought that if I could see more of you, then I could understand you." I laughed humorlessly. "I'm so used to my sisters telling me everything, and it infuriates me that I know practically nothing about you. The *real* you."

I felt him come up behind me, and thought I'd said too much, that he'd become angry again and try to hurt me. But then he whispered, in a low voice close to my ear, "I'd like to change that."

My heart sped up at his words and his nearness, but not because I was afraid. I couldn't understand the feeling that came over me then, and I didn't want to. I shook my clouded head as he came to stand in front of me, and instead of that hood there, I imagined an older version of the face of baby Bastian in the painting. Not the haughty prince I'd seen in the visions, but someone kinder, gentler.

His hood lowered a bit as his head bobbed towards me.

"Your hands," he growled, and I looked down. I'd almost completely forgotten about them, but as soon as he said it, they started to itch underneath their bandages.

I heard him swallow. "May I?" he asked quietly and I carefully held my hands out to him. I didn't know what he was going to do, but I knew I needed to gain his trust again, and that meant proving that I trusted him in return.

"For the record," he said, taking my trembling hands into his. I could feel the heat of him through the leather gloves that he wore, and I shivered. "I *am* sorry about last night. I've always had a bad temper, and as you can tell, I'm still quite vain despite all the time I've spent with this affliction. Sometimes I forget what it's like to be curious about someone."

"Are you curious about me?" I blurted out softly, and immediately regretted my words. I didn't even know why it mattered if he did.

His hands flinched beneath mine, but his voice sounded like he was smiling when he spoke again. "Of course. Now, close your eyes."

But they stayed open. I wasn't sure I trusted him enough for that yet.

"I won't hurt you," he assured me, and at that my eyes fell closed on their own.

He grasped my hands gently in his, and behind my eyelids a light grew. I wanted to open them to see what he was doing, but I reminded myself again that I needed to trust him. So, I kept completely still.

Then, suddenly, my hands stopped itching and the light began to dim. I waited.

"You can open them," he said in his gruff voice, and I did.

I unwrapped the bloody bandages from my right hand first, keeping my eyes on my palm. When the last piece of the bandage had fallen to the floor, I gasped at what was there: nothing, not even a scratch or a scar. I took off the other one quicker and saw the same thing. I didn't know black magic could do anything like this.

"I—how did you…" I shook my head. "I mean, thank you…" I trailed off, not sure what I should call him now. Him healing me—that was more intimate than anything I'd ever experienced. But it didn't feel right calling him Bastian.

"You can still call me the Beast," he told me like he knew what I was thinking, and I looked up at him in surprise. "I don't expect anything from you, Belle, and I haven't exactly proven my moniker to be false." He started to reach for me, but he must've decided better of it and dropped his hand back to his side. "You're a part of my home now, and if you'd ever like me to leave you alone, you only need to bid me gone. Anything you wish or desire, I am at your beck and call." He took a bold step towards me, but I didn't feel the urge to shy away. "Every day you spend here will be one more than I could've ever hoped for."

My lips parted in disbelief at the gentleness of his words, but I couldn't speak. He stayed for another moment before bowing and slipping past me. I didn't watch him go—I didn't want to think about what his words meant. And how they cut straight to my heart.

# CHAPTER 16

*Do Not Trust Too Much with Your Eyes*

<u>BASTIAN</u>

"WELL," SOPHIE prodded as soon as I entered the corridor to my chambers. "What happened? What did she say? What did *you* say? For heaven's sake, Bastian, speak!"

I chuckled, feeling lighter than I had in months—*years*. "You might not be as crazy as I thought, Soph." I sighed. "But I can't get my hopes up either."

"Of course you can," she sputtered, following me as I sat on my bed and shook off my hood. I went to smooth down my wild fur, but to no avail. For the millionth time, I wished that I could cut my mane, but each time Sophie or I had tried, it'd grown right back.

"She's the one. I can feel it," she said dreamily, as if Belle and I were in one of the epic love stories from the books in my library. But that would involve me being a handsome prince, and I was anything but.

"She likes you," she kept on, and I peered at her in surprise. Had Belle said something to her? "She just doesn't quite know it yet."

I scoffed. *Yeah, right.*

"Don't believe me?" she continued. "Check the mirror."

I shook my head. "I don't want to watch her when she can't see me. It doesn't seem right."

"Why?" she shrugged. "You did it every time you went near the village and she was out hunting."

"That's not the same thing and you know it," I growled.

She sighed. "Fine. But what if I look through first, to make sure she's not doing anything you shouldn't be seeing?"

The image of Belle undressing appeared in my head, her pulling the fitted gray sweater she'd had on in the greenhouse over her head, her golden-brown hair falling out of her loose bun in the process and catching in the sunlight—

I shook my head to dispel the fantasy. I couldn't think about her that way, not when she'd never think of *me* that way.

"Fine," I barked, but my tone didn't seem to affect Sophie; nothing did anymore.

She grinned triumphantly and hopped off where she'd been perched on the edge of my bed, pulling back the curtain next to it. There'd once been a window there, but after a few months of being the Beast, I'd replaced it with a mirror I'd made from my magic. I'd thought it might show me as my old self, without the fur and the scars. But I must've gotten the spell wrong because instead it showed everyone *but* me. As long as I knew the person's name, the mirror would show them, no matter where they were.

"Show me Belle Fairfax," Sophie commanded. The mirror flooded with purple smoke at her request, and I looked away as Belle's room came into view. It still felt wrong, and if she ever found out that I'd been watching her without her knowing, she might never speak to me again. But, as I'd admitted to her in the greenhouse, I was curious about her.

"Come look," Sophie told me, and my gaze snapped back to the mirror.

She was already in one of the only pair of pants I'd had Sophie leave in her room, though she'd kept the gray sweater on, her hair loose and flowing to mid-waist. I swallowed thickly; she was so beautiful it hurt to look at her.

Sitting on the edge of her bed, she was staring at her hands as if they no longer belonged to her. Painfully, I thought she might've regretted me healing them, but then she smiled slightly and stroked her thumb over her other palm. She looked...happy. But then she shook her head as confusion crept onto her face, dropping her hands into her lap before threading them through her hair in what looked like frustration.

I couldn't watch anymore.

I waved my hand at the mirror and her image was consumed by the purple smoke. Sophie didn't say anything, but I knew she was giving me a pitiful look. I put my head in my paws and she took that as her cue to leave.

Seeing Belle like that—so raw, unsure—made her more beautiful to me, and I now understood that I was in way over my head. I couldn't think of one solitary thing to get this girl to fall in love with me, and I was running out of time. My hopes of breaking the curse felt like they were slipping away.

# CHAPTER 17

*My Cruel Misery*

BELLE

I WAS in the middle of breakfast when the Beast joined me.

When I'd woken up this morning, my leg had felt infinitely better, and when Sophie had come to get me from my room, I'd asked her to help me out of the cast. I'd been unsteady on it first, and the skin underneath felt raw, but now there was very little pain. I thought about standing up to greet him, but he didn't seem to be in the mood for pleasantries.

His hood was up, still hiding his face from me, but his shoulders were more slumped than usual, and I wondered fleetingly if he'd slept well last night. I hadn't slept well either—I was curious about what had kept *him* awake.

"Morning," I said when I was done chewing. My voice echoed shrilly along the empty stones and I cringed at the sound. His head snapped up, and I didn't think he'd realized I was there because he straightened.

"Morning," he said back, unenthusiastically.

We were silent for some time after that, with only the sounds of our clanging dishware to fill the void, before I couldn't take it anymore.

"So," I began, pushing my eggs around my plate. The fork evidently didn't like that very much because it tried to carry a piece of the egg up to my mouth.

"I—I noticed the books in your room," I continued when I'd set the fork down. Maybe it wasn't the right thing to bring up so soon after it happened, but I wanted to know if they were pre-Regime. They had to be.

A smile in his voice as he said, "Yes, and…?"

"Are they…" I wasn't sure if he knew the phrase.

"Pre-Regime?" he guessed. I was surprised he knew it, considering the Regime hadn't started banning books until after they'd taken over Briar in his absence. "Yes, they *all* are."

"All?" I asked eagerly.

The Beast chuckled. "I'm guessing you read?"

I rolled my eyes at him, finding that I was grinning. "That's like asking a bird if it flies."

I imagined that he'd smiled in response. "Come with me."

He stood, but waited for me to follow. I shot up from my chair and bounded up to him. I was wearing a tighter pair of pants to keep my leg stable and the sweater from the day before, completely underdressed for dining with a king, but it didn't seem to bother the Beast. He held out his arm for me, and I took it without hesitation. The part of me that wanted to pull away from him was growing smaller with each passing day, and his warmth greeted me like an old friend as we started down another corridor I had yet to see.

This was the closest we'd been to each other since my coming here, and as the high ceilings of the dining hall disappeared into the lowered ones of the corridor, I felt heat crawling up my neck and splashing onto my cheeks. Why was I so nervous? It's not like I'd never been arm-in-arm with a boy before.

*But the Beast isn't a boy.*

In so many ways, he was unlike anyone I'd ever met. A part of me still blamed him for hiding away in his castle, and letting the Regime suffocate us in its corrupt hands. Another part was still afraid of him—of the Beast. But the man that was hidden beneath all the fur and jaded anger deserved to be seen, and I had to give him that chance.

We soon came to a large wooden door. The Beast pulled his arm away and my hand fell to my side. I eyed him curiously, hating the fact that I couldn't see the expression on his face, and watched as he moved behind me.

"What are you doing?" I asked.

He laughed low in his throat. "Don't worry, Belle. I'm just building up the suspense." I felt him move closer.

All I could do was swallow nervously.

He let out a throaty laugh before the door opened on its own, and I was met with a dark room.

My feet moved forward on their own accord, and he followed, our footsteps echoing louder than they had in the corridor. The air was cooler here, but the temperature of my skin remained hot. When I'd gone as far as I dared into the darkness, I stopped and so did the Beast.

For a moment, nothing happened and nervousness flitted around in my stomach. He came to stand beside me, and I heard a rustling of his cloak before floor-to-ceiling length drapes that matched the ones in the dining hall flew open—I couldn't help the gasp that escaped me.

It was a library. A vast and gorgeous library.

The shelves reached higher than I could see, and the room was a thousand times the size of Alinder's place. I moved towards the shelf nearest me and read the first spine I reached: *Paradise Lost* by John Milton. I stroked the brown leather once and sighed happily at the feeling of it beneath my fingertips.

"Oh," I breathed, and turned to the next book, and the next. *The Canterbury Tales* by Geoffrey Chaucer in green leather, *The Iliad* and *The Odyssey* by Homer both in red, *Grimm's Fairy Tales* in purple. I'd practically gone through all the titles at the bottom row of that first shelf when I remembered that the Beast was still there.

I turned around, seeing that he was in the same spot where I'd left him, his hands clasped behind his back. I approached him, forgetting the books for a moment.

Only a couple paces from him now, I asked, "Why do you always wear that hood?"

He didn't answer at first, and I began to wonder if he was going to answer at all, when he replied quietly, "I don't want to frighten you."

*I think that ship has sailed.* I thought about how he'd looked when he'd caught me in his room, how he hadn't been able to hide his features from me then. But I knew that wasn't the real Bastian. I knew now that there was so much more to him than that. His face *had* frightened me the last time I'd seen it, but this was different circumstances. This time, I was choosing to see him.

"I know it might seem hard to believe after the other night," I said, "but it takes a lot to scare me."

I reached for the top of his hood, but his paw caught my wrist. "Belle, don't…"

Without waiting for him to finish, my other hand shot up quickly and pushed back his hood before he could stop me.

The first thing I noticed once I looked past the fur was that his face was covered in scars; some silver like mine, others red and puckered like they'd never healed properly. There was a thin layer of fur covering them, but it didn't grow thick until his hairline, making him look like he was half wolf and half lion. His eyes, though—his eyes were impossibly blue. Like sapphires. They were the most human thing about him.

"I've seen worse," was my gut response, and I didn't realize I'd said it aloud until he let go of my wrist. My hand grabbed his arm gently before he could move away from me.

"Look," I said, and pointed at the silver scar on my cheek. "This runs all the way to my hip." I pulled down the neckline on my sweater to show where it spread out along my collarbone.

He looked away, huffing through his snout.

"I know what it's like to have scars," I continued on. "I can't count how many I have, and how much I hate every single one of them. But

I've learned that you can't let them define you. This," I said, gaze flitting across his face, "this isn't you."

He shook his head, refusing to look at me. "But it is, and I deserve it. I've deserved every moment of my punishment," he answered softly. "Do you not think me to be a hideous beast?"

I looked at him plainly. "There are plenty of other men in my life that merit the name beast more than you. You deserved to be cursed by the witch then, but not now. Bastian." I said his name—his real name—and he finally looked at me. Even though his face wasn't human, I could tell he was masking his emotions. I didn't care. He needed to hear this, even if it felt a little strange saying it to someone I thought I'd hated not long ago. "No one deserves this fate, not even you."

I brought my hand up to his face tentatively. When he didn't flinch or back away, I placed it on his cheek. His eyes fluttered closed and I stroked my thumb against the crevices in his skin. It was strange to me, to feel someone else's scars. He breathed out shakily as I pushed my fingers lightly through the fur by his temple—it was softer than I thought it would be.

A thought hit me then: this had become about more than just gaining his trust. More, even, than bringing a king back to life. Barring his single outburst, he was kind to me and thoughtful for bringing me to his library after learning that I loved to read, and his inability to hide his emotions endeared him more to me. I didn't hate him, not at all…

I jerked my hand back, which forced Bastian's eyes back open. *Oh no…* I turned away.

"I—I have to go," I mumbled, and I ran past him before he could say anything.

I expected him to call after me, or try to stop me, but he didn't. After racing back to my room and slamming my door shut, I couldn't believe how much I'd wanted him to.

# CHAPTER 18

*Deceived by Appearances*

BASTIAN

*W*HAT IN *the hell was that?* was all I could think after Belle
ran out of the library like a bat in the belfry. I hadn't been
touched like that since before I became the Beast, and it
had felt so foreign to me. It had felt...

"Sophie," I called, because I knew that, despite my requests, she was
waiting nearby.

Sure enough, she peeked around the corner of a slightly open
doorway that lead to the private study hidden at the back of the library.
She beamed for a moment, but when she looked around and realized Belle
wasn't there, she hurried over to me.

"What happened?" she demanded.

My fingers reached for the places she'd touched me. Her warmth lingered with me, and I thought about when she'd pulled back the neckline on her sweater to show me her scars, but all I'd seen was the creamy skin of her neck and shoulder.

"She saw my face," I told Sophie in wonder, and her eyes widened. "She *touched* my face, and she didn't hate it. Didn't hate *me*."

At that, I don't think her eyes could've gone any wider.

Then, she grinned. "This is the moment where I should say, 'I told you so,' but we have too much to do for me to have time to gloat." She launched into some long-winded explanation of what I should do, where I should take her, how I should look, how I should act. But I barely heard her.

"I'm taking her hunting tomorrow," I said after Sophie had finally stopped for air. I wasn't sure if that had been one of the things she'd just suggested, but when she didn't answer, I continued, "If I can get that reaction from her just bringing her to a *library*, then imagine what she might feel out in the forest, in the heat of the hunt."

But Sophie was already shaking her head. "She doesn't know that you spied on her, so how are you supposed to explain that you know she likes to hunt?"

I thought for a moment. "Well, we salvaged her bow and arrow that she had with her, so I could say I assumed that she hunted because of that."

Sophie sighed. "It's not a strong argument, but it'll do. When do you want me to relay your message?"

"Tomorrow, at dawn," I replied immediately. "I want her to be surprised."

Scoffing, she replied, "Nothing more romantic than getting up at the crack of dawn to hunt down some animals. But, since we have until tomorrow, *please* consider taking a bath." She moved closer to me and sniffed before pulling away, her nose wrinkling. "I'm honestly surprised she got close to you at all with how odorous you've become. Enchant one of the combs and half a dozen bottles of shampoo. That should just about do it." Then she turned on her heel and walked away.

I wanted to protest, but I took a whiff of myself and realized she was right.

But nothing was going to dampen my mood. Peering up at the high shelves of my library, I couldn't help the toothy smile that formed on my face. The hope growing in my heart—it was intoxicating.

And dangerous.

# CHAPTER 19

## Destined for a Better Fate

### BELLE

I SLEPT fitfully that night, going over and over in my head what had possessed me to be so bold with the Beast—*Bastian*. There was no denying that I was starting to care for him, but I couldn't let that get it in the way of what I had to do. I still needed to get the ring. I still needed to save my sisters.

But maybe I didn't have to steal it from him anymore. Maybe now we could come to some sort of agreement.

No, I could already see the betrayal in his eyes. The betrayal would be there no matter what I did, but I was selfish and it would hurt too much to see it for myself. This was going to wound both of us in the end, and I wasn't sure I could care for Bastian the way he needed me to. What if he turned out to still be the spoiled prince he once was, or the terrible king who'd gotten himself cursed? It would be almost worse than marrying Thomas. But I had to believe that Bastian had been through too much to revert back to his former self.

My mind was far too busy for sleep.

It was in the early hours of the morning when I was woken up by a knock at my door, after finally drifting off. I grumbled something unintelligible and pulled the sheets over my head; I was getting used to their silky feeling and the weight of the fur comforter in the cold parts of the night. The knock came louder a minute later when I was nearly asleep again, and I growled as I pulled myself out of bed, hair sticking sideways, clothing askew, and answered the door.

It was Sophie, as I'd expected, and I glared at her. But she didn't seem to notice.

"Bastian wishes to see you," she said calmly. Her eyes were devoid of sleep, her uniform unwrinkled. She looked wide awake and I was completely envious.

"Now?" I asked groggily, rubbing at my eyes. Not that I wasn't used to getting up before the sun rose, but not when I'd gotten as little sleep as I had.

Sophie smiled. "Against my recommendations, yes." She looked me over. "Wear something warm and comfortable. You're going outside the castle today. I suggest pants and the black tunic." And then she left.

I closed the door slowly and leaned against it, lost in my sleep-filled mind. *Outside the castle?* I wondered why Bastian wanted to go outside the castle. But it didn't matter why. At the thought of being outside, I had a sudden urge to run as fast as I could—not to anywhere in particular, but now that I think thinking about it, I felt confined inside this place. I'd been trying so hard on getting the ring, while avoiding being killed by the Beast I'd thought Bastian was, that I hadn't noticed how much the castle walls were restricting me.

The openness of the greenhouse hadn't been enough.

I wondered if Bastian knew how I was feeling or if he simply wanted to spend time with me outside these stone walls. Probably a little of both.

Standing in the middle of this room that had become mine, I tried to understand why I seemed to mean so much to him. Why my opinion of him mattered. I knew that the stories said he needed a girl to fall in love with him to break the spell, but if it was true, it felt like more than that. He couldn't know why I was here unless Sophie had told him, yet I was sure he'd guessed by now that I wasn't staying because I wanted to. And while my feelings towards him had started to change, I'd leave the moment the ring was in my possession. My first priority was to keep my sisters safe. Nothing else was going to get in the way of that.

I slipped on the pants and a new black tunic like Sophie had suggested, tying my hair back loosely. It revealed more of my scar, but I got the feeling Bastian wouldn't care. And for once, neither did I.

I found some black riding boots in the back of the closet and was amazed that they fit, though that probably had something to do with magic, like everything else in this place. I reached into what was left of my pack—which I'd nearly forgotten was there—and pulled out my leather jacket. There was a small tear in the arm where the elbow was but otherwise it was in good shape. This was one of the few times that I wished there was a mirror in my room, even knowing why there weren't any. I tended to avoid mirrors as well, but I wanted to look at myself, to know which version of me Bastian would like more: the girl in a gown at dinners, the girl underdressed for a king and infatuated with every book in the library, or the girl who wore hunting pants and loved being out in the woods.

*Does it really matter?*

I sighed as I zipped up my jacket, feeling like I was being torn in two different directions by my feelings.

Stepping outside of my room, I found Sophie waiting for me. She didn't speak, and there was a small smile on her lips that seemed permanent now. Wordlessly, we again swept through the dining room and I was finding it easier to walk today, my broken leg less unsteady beneath me.

"Are we seeing the roses again today?" I asked as we turned down what I now knew to be the corridor towards the greenhouse, but Sophie didn't answer. I wasn't sure why that put me on-edge, my muscles tensing unconsciously.

The glass doors to the greenhouse were closed, but Sophie wrenched them open with a screech. At first, I couldn't see anything—the sun wasn't up yet, and the room was filled with shadows. Then, rays of sunlight peeked over the nearby mountains and in through the green glass, casting everything in an emerald glow.

And there was Bastian, appearing out of the darkness like a phantom. I took a few steps towards him without thinking, and then decided to go the rest of the way. He wasn't wearing his hood today, and his mane actually looked tame for once.

*Did he do this for me?* I wondered.

He was wearing all black to match me, his blond mane contradicting his clothes in a way that made my breath stutter in my lungs.

When he heard me coming, he turned slightly, smiled close-lipped, and offered me his arm. I took it. His cobalt eyes caught the sun, and I stopped breathing altogether. They really were striking...

"Good morning, Belle."

"This feels like the middle of the night for me," I admitted, grinning tiredly. "There'd better be a good reason why I'm up this early."

He chuckled. "Of course there is. But, first, I wanted to show you the greenhouse at sunrise. It's the most beautiful room in the entire castle at this time of day."

I looked around us, and the contrast of the green light and green plants against the red of the roses was stunning. I reached toward one of the blooms, and Bastian must've used a bit of magic because it bended on its own to meet me, my finger brushing against the velvet of the petals.

But when I looked over at him, his expression was one of confusion.

"What's wrong?" I asked.

"The roses never do that for anyone but me," he said, pausing thoughtfully. "Did you cut yourself on one of the thorns?"

I thought of the first time that I'd come here with Sophie, and vaguely recalled pricking my finger. I nodded, still not sure what that had to do with this rose moving on its own.

Bastian smiled, almost as if he didn't believe it. "The roses recognize you, Belle. They know when you're near because they've had a taste of your blood."

I pulled back from the rose and it seemed to wilt. "That's not comforting at all."

He looked down at me. "They completely harmless."

I rolled my eyes. "I know that, it's just—a little unsettling."

"Fear not," he told me gallantly. "I'll keep the murderous roses at bay."

I laughed. "Now I feel safe."

His gloved hand brushed my arm. "Come with me; it's time for your second surprise today."

I looked at him, but didn't move, not sure what I wanted. Going outside the castle walls with Bastian suddenly felt like we were going past the point of no return, and I didn't think I was ready.

He peered back at me. "Do you trust me?"

The question caught me off guard, and it took me a moment to answer. "I want to."

"I want that too," he said quietly, smiling sadly as he started down the castle corridor, and I followed.

We left the green room, taking our time finding our way back through the dining hall and down a corridor I thought I remembered but couldn't be sure. This one was short and wide, and it wasn't long until we reached a high-ceilinged entryway ending in two large doors. Bastian flicked his wrist and they swung inward, revealing spikes on the other side. I eyed them warily as we passed through, but Bastian seemed completely at ease.

New snow coated the castle grounds, nearly blinding me as the sunlight reflected off it. It was beautiful.

*What are we doing out here?*

Wordlessly, he left my side and went over to retrieve a couple of packs that were waiting on top of the thick layer of snow, holding one out for me. Watching the tops of my feet sink into the snow as I moved towards him and grabbed one of the straps, I was glad I chose to wear the riding boots.

He grinned at me, teeth and all, and I didn't have the urge to pull back when I saw how sharp they were. "Here, this is yours." He handed me my bow and quiver, which he'd filled with black-feathered arrows. I took it from him, unsure. *Is he taking me hunting?*

Before I could ask, he took off, striding purposefully towards the Black Forest, and I hurried along after him, finding his arm again where he held it out for me. I didn't have the best memories of this forest, and I had to admit I was anxious about what might happen. But having Bastian with me made me feel safe.

In the silence, I watched our breaths cloud the air in front of us, his was bigger than mine.

We walked further down the path, and as the cold set into my bones, I moved closer to him. I thought I heard a sound low in his throat, but was sure I'd imagined it.

Looking around, a strange color caught my eye and, despite the snow that coated the ground, I noticed that the land was bursting with fruits and vegetables. It was such a contrastingly beautiful thing, seeing life like that in the dead of winter, and I was again struck by the power of Bastian's magic.

"I thought you could use some time outside of the castle," he explained as we walked through a wrought iron gate and past the tree line of the forest. I ripped my gaze away from where it had landed on a goldenapple tree, the skin of the fruit sparkling in the sunlight.

"You have no idea," I replied, but then felt a twinge of guilt of how that must've sounded.

Bastian just chuckled. "Believe me, I do. For the first year after I was cursed with this"—he gestured to himself—"I locked myself inside my room and refused to even look out a window." He shook his head, remembering, but he didn't look sad. He looked thoughtful—pensive. Despite his indifference to it, those must've been dark times for him.

I didn't want to flesh out old wounds, but I was curious. "How long ago did it happen?"

Bastian sighed, and then stopped. I turned to stand in front of him, keeping my hand on his arm. It felt natural. "It'll be five years on February 5th."

That was only a few days away. "Is it—" I began, but the words stuck in my throat at first and I forced myself to clear it.

"Is the story true?" I asked finally. "All of it?"

Bastian looked down at me and pinned me with an intense gaze. "Every word, I'm sure."

For no reason at all, my eyes strayed to his cheeks, his snout, his jaw, and then back to his eyes. I caught his own gaze drifting to my lips, and he swallowed before he moved towards me. But I stepped back, dropping my hand from his arm, and looked up at the trees. The sounds of the forest found their way to my ears, and I remembered why we were out here.

I crossed my arms and turned back to him as he looked away, disappointment flashing across his face before it disappeared. Mutely, he headed towards the trunk of a tree, where I saw a wooden pole propped up against the snowy bark. It looked like one of the ones from his weapon room—he must've put it out here earlier. Grabbing it with one hand, he came back towards me.

My arms uncrossed and fell to my sides. "What are you doing?"

"Teaching you something," he told me surreptitiously, and handed the pole to me. I held it awkwardly until he'd positioned it in my hands to where I was holding it with both palms facing down and my knuckles were pointing out.

"As I'm sure you remember, the Black Forest is dangerous, but not just because of the Forest Wolves," he explained. "Bandits and thieves from other Regime territories have taken to hiding here to avoid being captured and put to death. I don't often run into them, but it never hurts to be prepared."

I waited for him to continue, and he asked me softly, "Remember how you said that you wanted to trust me?"

"Yes," I said; I was sure he could hear the uncertainty in my voice.

"Well," he continued as he walked behind me, coming up close, "Let me show you that you can."

Without warning, both of his gloved paws shot out to grip the underside of my wrists. I flinched at the sudden movement, but only because I hadn't expected it, not that I was afraid of what he might do.

"Now," he began, his chest moving against my back as he breathed deeply, and I found myself taking the breath with him, "do as I do."

I was so distracted by the way his body warmed mine in the cold that it took me a moment to notice the thing that had taken shape before me.

At first, there was only this strange purple smoke, curling through the winter air. As it floated apart, there appeared a faceless, featureless figure that looked just as real as Bastian or I, dipped in black from head to toe.

"The figure will try to attack us, when I give the command," Bastian murmured into my ear. "Let me lead you first, and then you'll be on your own."

The figure then let out an inhuman shriek and flew at us, a similar pole suddenly in its grasp. I recoiled into Bastian's chest, unsure of what was happening, but his hold on me never wavered, and we met the black phantom head-on.

Together, we blocked its first advance, and then its second, and for a few moments, it felt like Bastian and I were the same person. At first, we only dodged the strikes, but he began to move against the figure until we had the upper hand. I'd never felt this before—this rush of the fight. Of getting the best of a skilled opponent. It made me feel strong, powerful.

It was then that he let me go.

At first, I felt unbalanced, and though it seemed like the figure was giving me a chance to get my bearings, its tightening grip on the pole told me it was growing impatient. Then, it rushed me. Instinctively, I turned the end of the pole towards it just in time to block down the thrust. No longer having Bastian's strength behind me caused a quick pain to shoot up my arms from the impact.

"Trust your instincts," Bastian called out to me, and I shook my head to clear it—*I can do this.*

Taking a forward stance, I didn't wait for the figure to come at me again. I lunged forward and swung down with my left arm, watching as it sidestepped my move easily. It came at me again, with greater force than before, and our poles met jarringly. Taking a step back, I stumbled over something hard and jagged beneath the snow, and without Bastian behind me, I felt myself tumbling backward.

The figure disappeared as quickly as it had come and Bastian's arms caught me before I could hit the ground. I looked up at him through tangled wisps of my hair that had come loose and saw that he was trying to hide a smile.

"Sorry about that," he said, lifting me so that I could stand on my own again. "The magic is a bit tricky with them. They can sometimes form a mind of their own."

I snorted out a laugh, still a bit shaken. "Sure they can."

Bastian looked offended. "You can't think that was on purpose."

I shrugged, trying not to grin in return. "I mean, it's *your* magic, after all."

He shook his head, then looked back up at me with a hooded gaze. "You did very well, Belle."

I bowed theatrically, a wide smile seeming to be plastered permanently on my face now. Catching my bow and arrow out of the corner of my eye, though, suspicion grew in my mind.

"How did you know that I like to hunt?" I asked, folding my arms across my chest.

Bastian shrugged. "I found you with a bow and arrow and callouses on your fingers, so I assumed you at least used the thing once or twice."

"So it *was* you that saved me that night," I said, though I'd guessed the answer a while ago. I just wanted to hear him admit it.

He smiled, and I was sure he could tell that I'd already figured it out. "Don't let it go to your head. I would've done it for anyone."

"I doubt that," I said—that got his attention. "You were obviously so entranced by my unmistakable beauty that you couldn't bear to see me ripped apart by the forest wolves."

Bastian laughed fully, a rumbling sound that I liked instantly. "Yes, that must've been it. Though your beauty, while certainly entrancing, wasn't what helped me find you."

I froze. He'd called me beautiful, though I wasn't sure he'd realized it. No one had said that to me since my scars.

"And what was that?" I managed.

"You were practically trampling through the forest. A deaf squirrel could've found you."

I scoffed and shook my head at him in disbelief, stepping towards him to push at his chest lightly. He pretended to stumble back, clutching at his heart, and I laughed.

After a beat, he said, "I come out here to hunt the wolves that my magic has created. Sometimes, the younger ones are feeling bold and they come find me. But the older ones are smarter."

"Why do you hunt them?" I asked, searching the forest for any sign of the creatures.

"Because I created the monsters, and the least I can do is kill as many as I can." Bastian shrugged. "Besides, they're easy for me to take down, even without a weapon."

I lifted an eyebrow at him. "Bit cocky, aren't we?"

"Fine, don't believe me?" He gestured up. "Climb that tree and wait.

You'll see."

I stared at him a moment, but did as he said. The branches on the tree were perfectly placed for me to climb, and even though my body was still stiff from my injuries, I was able to do it.

As soon as I'd climbed up high enough in the tree, I sat on a solid-looking branch and waited. Bastian looked up at me and grinned toothily. Then he closed his eyes, opened his mouth, and howled so loud that I had to cover my ears. It was deep and piercing—my whole body vibrated from it.

He cut off a few seconds later, and the forest answered with silence.

Alert now, my sharpened gaze roved over the trees and the ground below, and I opened all of my senses to the woods. Not long after, I heard the soft crunch of paws on snow. I pulled out an arrow silently and placed it in my bow. Glancing down at Bastian, I saw that he was crouched in an attack position, facing where I'd heard the wolf, teeth bared. He looked dangerous and a lot like the night he'd caught me in his room. But at least his anger wasn't directed at me this time.

The young wolf entered the small clearing, ears back, tail low, its black coat thick and wet from the snow. It growled at Bastian and I tensed, training my arrow on the pup. I was sure Bastian could handle himself, but I wanted to be sure nothing would go wrong. The young wolves may not have had the experience, but they had stamina on their side. Sometimes youth won out over skill—I'd make sure that didn't happen.

Just as I thought this, the young wolf leapt at Bastian, teeth bared. He moved at the last moment in a blur, the creature barreling past him, and I let out the breath I didn't realize I'd been holding. Without hesitating, the wolf turned back and charged him again. This time, Bastian stood his ground. I wanted to yell at him to move, but I had to remind myself that he knew what he was doing. He held his paws out and let the wolf fall on top of him. I straightened up and pulled my arrow back, closing one eye. A few more seconds and I would—

Suddenly, Bastian was on top of the wolf instead. He pinned its paws to its chest, and though the wolf had its sharp teeth bared at him, Bastian simply head-butted the creature, effectively knocking it out. Then he took the wolf's head in his ungloved hands and twisted its neck with a resounding crack.

I swallowed hard. Despite the callousness of the kill, I knew that the hybrid wolves were dangerous, and Bastian hated himself for creating them. At least he was doing something about it.

I dropped down from the tree into the snow. Bastian still had his back to me, looking down at the wolf. "Impressive," I commented.

"See, I told you," he said breathlessly. When he turned around to look at me, I saw the blood and gasped. He had a long gash across his forehead and three claw marks down his left side shown only by the torn fabric.

"Are you okay?" I demanded loudly, and he looked down at himself, as if just realizing that he was hurt.

"This?" he gestured to himself. "Don't worry, it's just a flesh wound. Now get back up in that—" But his words were cut off by a large flash of black fur flying into him and knocking him to the ground.

"Bastian!" I called out as the new wolf growled on top of him.

This wolf was much bigger that the first, his claws shredding through Bastian's clothes and fur like butter, burying into his skin. He cried out;

the sound felt wrong and my stomach dropped.

Bastian was dying.

It opened its jaw to bite into Bastian's neck, and, on instinct, I brought up my bow which had been loose at my side, pulled back the arrow dangling between my fingers and released it. Swiftly, it imbedded itself into the roof of the wolf's mouth, and the impact forced it backwards into the snow. It twitched a couple of times before becoming still.

Almost as still as Bastian…

I just stared at him a moment, not believing what had happened, looking for a sign that he was alive. Then, his chest moved up and down as he fought to breathe, and a sob caught in my throat.

He was alive—for now.

I ran to him, sinking into the snow beside his broken body. His chest and stomach were bleeding profusely—blood seeped into the snow, staining it red. "Bastian? Bastian!"

He opened his eyes and I exhaled in relief. "See," he said hoarsely. "Just a flesh wound." Then he coughed, and blood spattered his lips, speckling the snow with flecks of crimson.

I shook my head at him, touching his face gently. "I have to get you to Sophie."

He tried to pull himself to his knees, groaning. I worried that he might attract more wolves, but there was nothing I could do about that. I grabbed onto the arm with less blood on it and used any strength I had to haul him up. He began falling to one side and I braced myself against a tree to keep him upright.

"Can you walk?" I asked. He answered me by hobbling one painful step at a time out of the woods and through the gate towards the castle.

We nearly fell to the ground a couple of times, but finally reached the open doors. Sophie was waiting there, looking suspiciously unsurprised at what she was seeing.

"He was attacked," I told her breathlessly.

Without answering, she took hold of his other side and together we brought him inside the doors. I heard them close resolutely as we left them behind, cutting off the early-morning sunlight that had bled into the castle.

"We'll take him to the infirmary," she said finally.

Not sure where that was exactly, I let Sophie lead and helped steer Bastian down the right corridor, past the room where I slept. He was putting more and more weight on us, and by the time we got him to a cot, he fell into it. There was a path of red blood trailing into the room and now pooling beneath the cot. He was losing too much…

"Sophie," I warned.

"Don't worry, Belle. This happens at least half a dozen times in a year." But she looked too worried for that to be true.

"How bad is it?" I asked.

She took her eyes off him and found mine for a moment. "I don't know," she answered honestly, then hurried off into another room.

She came back a moment later with a container of what looked like milky water that had been frozen over, but the smell told me it was the stuff she'd put on my hands. Skipping the cloth she'd used before, she took off the top and tipped it over his chest and stomach; I cringed as the whole of it hit his skin in globs. He roared, and then fell back into the cot in silence. He must've passed out.

I couldn't take being so far away from him when he was in such pain. I rushed over and knelt close enough that I could hold his hand, not caring about the blood and burning liquid that touched me. His skin was horribly cold and my throat tightened. This couldn't be it. There had to be more time.

I bowed my head, hot tears slicing down my winter-bitten cheeks. Then I gripped his hand tighter and willed him to live.

# CHAPTER 20

## She Would Be Alone

BASTIAN

**M**Y HEAD swam like I'd had too much wine when I woke—
and then the pain slammed into me.

It consumed me completely, and my entire body was on
fire before the flames settled into my chest and stomach. I
went to clench my fists to keep the pain at bay, but there was something
in one of them. I opened my eyes, and though my vision was blurry, I
could see a small figure laid out next to me on the bed.

*Belle.*

She was alright; she was *alive.* I thought I'd killed us both when I'd
forgotten to check if there were more wolves nearby. I'd let the kill go to
my head and had almost died because of it—had almost gotten Belle killed
too.

As I'd laid there helplessly, waiting for the wolf to kill me, I'd heard something cutting swiftly through the air and then the wolf falling to snowy ground, an arrow in its mouth. She'd saved me.

And she was in a bed, with me...

With my other hand, I felt the sheets beneath me and knew that I was in my own bed in my chambers, and not in one of the cots in the infirmary. I remembered being there briefly, but I had no recollection of being moved here. Sophie and Belle must've worked together to carry me here. Moving my legs to reposition myself, I looked down and noticed that my entire torso was wrapped in bandages; I was also in different pants than the ones I'd had on.

Even though it was probably Sophie who'd dressed me, a different kind of heat rose to my cheeks.

I turned to peer over at Belle. Her hair had fallen out of her ponytail and it spilled out around her, a few strands caught in the light from the single flame that lit the room. Her face was slightly strained, her skin cinched even in sleep, but still unbearably beautiful. She was wearing the same clothes she'd worn out hunting, the fabric covered in dried blood. Had she stayed with me this entire time? How long had I been unconscious?

I went to move onto my side to get a better view of her, but my body screamed in pain. I let out an inhuman groan and Belle stirred. She opened her eyes lazily, saw me looking at her, and shot up.

"Are you alright?" she asked worriedly, her fingers barely grazing the bandages over my shredded skin.

I awkwardly caught one of her hands and she stilled. "I'm fine," I assured her. Her eyes narrowed at me and I could tell she didn't believe me. I tried to smile without grimacing, and that seemed to satisfy her. She laid back down next to me slowly, continuing to eye me with worry.

"Stop looking at me like that," I told her, my voice barely over a whisper; I felt like I hadn't used it in days. "You're making me feel like I'm going to die any moment."

She gave me a watery smile, until it melted into worry again. "You very nearly did," she answered tightly.

I didn't answer her. Watching the way her face changed as she looked at me, I suddenly felt like I was drowning in the possibility that she loved me. After nearly getting mauled to death by one of my own creations, I could tell that she cared whether I lived or died. Maybe even more than that.

And the thing was, I was falling for her again, this Belle that I knew now. I thought I'd loved the Belle that I'd seen out hunting in the forest, who muttered under her breath and sometimes hummed a sad tune on the way back to her cottage, who selflessly took care of her sisters. But this Belle that I'd come to know…I loved her more than I'd ever loved anyone.

I didn't even care anymore if she broke the curse. I was so deeply enthralled with her that I'd do anything just to be near her. Anything.

At that thought, my eyes started to fall closed as unconsciousness pulled at me.

"Sleep," she said, and I did.

# CHAPTER 21

## *If She Could Not Be Happy*

### BELLE

A S SOON as Bastian closed his eyes and I heard his breathing become more even, I moved to lay on my back, putting my fingers up to my lips in thought.

Seeing Bastian almost die had brought things into perspective: I needed to know if my sisters were alright.

I'd wait however long it took for Bastian to heal properly, and then I'd ask him to come with me back to town. I didn't even need to speak with my sisters; I just needed to know that they hadn't been carted off to the Brothel yet, or taken under Thomas' control, or left at the market by father. So many things could've gone wrong in all this time, and here I was, completely fixated on myself. Not thinking for one moment that they were having a worse time from this deal than I was. It no longer surprised me that Bastian had been able to keep to himself in this place, ignoring the outside world.

I wondered what my sisters were doing right now. I couldn't even remember what day of the week it was, but I was sure Em was on her way to her job at the dairy by now, with Lila in tow after picking her up from Mrs. Larue's. I could see them walking there, swinging their arms back and forth, laughing at something Lila had said.

My chest ached from not being with them.

I peered back at Bastian. He was still turned towards me, his lips parted slightly, his face slack. He looked almost serene and I wondered if he dreamed…

"Belle," a voice called, and I realized I'd fallen asleep again as my eyes flew open.

It had been Bastian that had called my name, but he seemed calm, not in pain. He still hadn't moved, though he was wearing a loose tunic now. I managed a smile.

"Bastian." But even I could hear the sadness in my voice, and I knew he'd notice.

Worry brought down his scarred brow. "What's wrong?"

I waved it away. I couldn't tell him about wanting to see my sisters just yet. He'd probably try to leave with me right this moment, and he needed to heal.

"Nothing," I told him. "How are you feeling?"

He eyed me a moment longer, as if he knew I was keeping something from him, but when he tried to turn to me, he winced in pain.

I sat up. "Sophie!" I called out, as she told me she'd be nearby.

She came through the doors quickly and immediately went to Bastian. "What is it?" she demanded.

"I think it's his bandages," I explained. "They've likely stuck to the wounds by now."

Sophie nodded and lifted up the clean shirt she must've put on him earlier. Blood and puss had bled through the bandages and I reached for him without thinking, then pulled back as Sophie began unwrapping them. It looked bad, but I tried to keep the worry off my face. Luckily, Bastian had closed his eyes again, so he couldn't see me.

Once the bandages were gone, I saw that the gashes were deeply imbedded into his skin. His chest and stomach had miraculously begun to heal themselves, but it still looked gruesome.

Now Bastian was watching me.

"One of these days, you're going to get yourself killed with your stupidity," Sophie grumbled, and both Bastian and I cracked a smile at her curmudgeonly state.

"Only with your permission, Soph," Bastian replied, though his voice was still hoarse.

Sophie scoffed. "Don't try to charm your way out of this one, boy." She began applying the salve and Bastian sighed in relief. "I'm still angry with you."

He laughed once, though it was more like a cough. "Fair enough."

Sophie paused for a moment, then looked at me. "Can you leave us for a moment?"

I met her fuming gaze, then glanced at Bastian. He looked just as confused as I felt. But I nodded and got up from the bed, not taking my eyes off him until I'd closed the door. Then, I waited, refusing to move even though the chill from the night clung to the castle stones and swept deep underneath my skin.

A little while later, I finally heard voices behind the door. Sophie was the first to speak, and her words came out like venom.

"How could you have been so stupid?"

Silence.

"I lost focus," Bastian said finally.

"You could've been killed," she practically growled.

"But I wasn't," he argued.

"Yes, thanks to Belle. Tell me the truth: would you have lived if she hadn't killed that wolf?"

How did she know about that? Had she been watching Bastian and I in the clearing? And if she'd been there and seen us, why hadn't she come to help?

There was a long pause before Bastian answered, defeated. "No."

Another silence. "Don't ever risk yourself like that again, especially for some girl. I've seen you almost die too many times."

I heard footsteps coming toward the door and bolted to my room. But I couldn't help wondering if that had been the end of the conversation.

~

Another day passed while Bastian continued to heal. I kept to my room mostly; after overhearing the conversation between him and Sophie, I got the feeling I wasn't wanted. And the old woman hadn't come by once to contradict it, or to ask me to come see Bastian. Selfishly, I wondered if he was asking for me.

It was the second night since the wolf attack, and I was getting restless. I wanted to check on Bastian, to make sure he was alright. But he was also the only way I was going to be able to see my sisters. If anyone could navigate the Black Forest, it was him.

I knew he needed time, though. When he was feeling better, he'd come to me.

The fireplace had lit itself after the sun went down a few hours ago, and I sat in front of it, staring into the flames but not really seeing them. Instead, I kept seeing the wolf on top of Bastian, tearing away a piece of his life with each slash of its claws. What if I hadn't known how to shoot an arrow, or I'd frozen up from fear? Bastian would be dead.

I shivered at the thought despite the warmth of the fire.

A knock at my door made me flinch, the sound harsh on my ears after more than a day alone with only my thoughts. I picked myself off the ground stiffly, and opened the door, expecting to find Sophie.

But to my surprise, it was Bastian. My face flushed—he'd never come to my door before.

Slightly slumped, he stood in the threshold, gripping a silver tray with two plates of food. I quickly took the weight of it from him. He was wearing the black pants he always seemed to have on and a navy-blue sweater that was stretched out, probably from before he'd become the Beast. It also looked like Sophie had made him take a bath again, because his hair was wet and slicked back. His gaze was downcast—I had the urge to put my arms around him. It felt like it had been an eternity since I'd seen him last.

"Come in," I said.

He barely lifted his head as he moved into the room, and he wouldn't meet my eyes. I set the tray down by the fire. Looking back at him, I gestured towards the rug on the floor and sat. He came to sit beside me, and I peered at him in confusion, cocking my head to the side so that he would look at me. But he ignored me, pushing his food around with the long claw of one of his fingers.

"What's wrong?" I asked.

He stopped playing with his dinner and finally looked up at me. "Aren't you angry with me?"

"Angry? Why would I be angry?" I wondered, picking up my fork, trying to prove to him that nothing was wrong. That everything was fine, even if I wasn't sure that it was.

Bastian stared at me. "I almost got you killed."

"No, you almost got *yourself* killed," I amended. "In fact, I saved your sorry hide."

He eyed me like I had two heads. I laughed softly. "Look, Bastian, I'm not Sophie. She's practically your mother the way she frets about you. I care about you," I continued, and his eyes widened, as if he was seeing me for the first time tonight, "but I know that you can take care of yourself. If I hadn't been there, you would've heard the second wolf and taken it down easily. But I *was* there, and I was able to kill the wolf that I'd distracted you from in the first place." I shook my head. "Why would I be *mad* at you?"

"Well," he said, leaning back slightly, "when you say it like that, it sounds almost...logical." He paused. "Thank you, for saving me."

I grinned. "I guess we're even now."

He grinned back toothily, and I looked down at my food. I was starving, but my stomach was in knots. At first, I couldn't understand why…then I realized Bastian and I were alone in my room. I glanced back up at him, and saw that he'd come to the same conclusion. He reached a paw to grip the back of his furry neck.

"I brought you something," he said, pulling out a thick book from his back pants pocket.

I smiled, biting my lip. "Which book is it?"

"Hamlet," he answered softly, and I drew in a breath.

I loved Hamlet more than any of the bard's other plays; it was the first Shakespearean work Alinder had read to me. While my mother had always enjoyed the love-sick tale of Romeo and Juliet, I'd wanted to read more about murder and betrayal and lost love.

"Hamlet is one of my favorites," I said instead.

He deflated. "Oh, you've already read it," he replied, and then grumbled, "Of course you have."

I touched his arm. "Please read to me."

He looked down at my hand on his arm, and when I didn't move it, he swallowed. "Alright."

I scooted beside him as he took the play in his hands. "Do you have a favorite part?" he asked.

I smiled, remembering Alinder reading it to me in all the different voices. "Yes, the graveyard scene."

He scoffed. "That's the only scene people know. 'Alas, poor Yorick!— I knew him, Heratio'," he mimicked in a high voice. Or, at least as high as his voice could go, which made it sound even more ridiculous.

I laughed outright. "Not that speech, the one just after it. Go to that scene and I'll show you."

He flipped almost directly to the page, as if he'd done it a million times. I moved closer and my fingers skimmed the small font until I found it. "There," I pointed.

He read silently to where I'd shown him, a smile forming on his lips when he spoke the words aloud. "'No, faith, not a jot; but to follow him thither with modesty enough, and likelihood to lead it: as thus; Alexander died, Alexander was buried, Alexander returneth into dust; the dust is earth: of earth we make loam; and why of that loam whereto he was converted might they not stop a beer-barrel? Imperious Ceasar, dead and turn'd to clay, Might stop a hole to keep the wind away: O, that' that earth which kept the world in awe Should patch a wall t'expel the winter's flaw!— '"

Bastian stopped, and chuckled. "Hamlet can never just say anything simply, can he?"

I was about to agree, but the memory of why that passage spoke to me so deeply came into my head, and I sobered. "I read that passage just after my mother died. She would've wanted to be with the dust and dirt. That's where she always was anyway..."

I dropped my head to Bastian's shoulder as I trailed off. His warmth comforted me. He tentatively brought his arm around me, draping it across my shoulders, and placing his hand on my arm. I shivered and moved closer to him. A single tear slipped down my cheek and onto his sweater, but I didn't wipe it away.

"What's your favorite part?" I asked, trying to hide my tears. But the thickness in my voice gave it away.

Bastian didn't speak at first, and I thought he wasn't going to answer. Then he said, "On the next page."

I closed my eyes. "Read it to me," I whispered.

I heard him turn the page and clear his throat, "'I loved Ophelia: forty-thousand brothers could not, with all their quantity of love, make up my sum.—What wilt thou do for her?'" He paused skipping over the quick lines of the king and queen. It comforted me that he understood the play well enough to know that those lines didn't matter. That Hamlet wouldn't have heard them anyway. "'"Swounds, show me what thou'lt do: Woo't weep? woo't fight? woo't fast? woo't tear thyself? Woo't drink up eisel? eat a crocodile? I'll do't.—Dost thou come here to whine? To outface me with leaping in her grave? Be buried quick with her, and so will I.'" He stopped there, though I knew that wasn't the end of the speech.

I opened my eyes and sat up slightly to see him looking at me. His blue eyes were burning into mine, but I didn't look away. "I was always fascinated by that passage because I've never known that feeling—to love someone so completely that you'd be willing to die a thousand agonizing deaths for them." He paused, glancing away. "But…I think I'm beginning to understand what Hamlet meant."

My breath caught in my throat, and I moved away from him, unable to take the emotion that had overcome me. He was practically telling me that he loved me and I just… I didn't know to say. I didn't even know how I felt.

We were silent for a heartbreaking moment before he spoke, "I want to show you something."

I swallowed hard, nodding for him to continue, though I still couldn't look at him.

He cleared his throat again, and the awkwardness in the room was nearly tangible. "Sophie told me not to do any more surprises with you, but I couldn't resist this time."

Fighting back a smile, I turned to him. "We're not taking a trip into the forest at night, are we? Due to previous experience, I'm going to have to turn down such an offer."

Bastian chuckled in a husky voice, the moment when I'd pulled away seemingly forgotten. "Nothing like that," he assured me. "Do you trust me?"

"Yes," I said without hesitation this time.

Bastian stood up and held out his hand for me. "Then come with me."

Leaving the food and Hamlet on the floor, I took his paw. I felt his eyes on me as we walked out of my room, and I couldn't help glancing over to meet them before turning away. There was something different about tonight, but I couldn't quite put my finger on what it was.

Quickly, we passed through the dining room and into another part of the castle, coming to the entrance of a large, high-ceilinged room. It was circular and lit by candlelight, with a piano and several other instruments stuffed into one of the shadowy corners. The walls around us were trimmed in gold and…mirrors. The entire bottom quarter of the room was lined with them. They were a bit dusty and faded, but they were there. I let go of his hand, stepping closer to one of the mirrors to get a look at myself. I hadn't seen my reflection in days, though it felt like months. I never realized before how often I looked at my appearance despite always trying to avoid it.

"Why didn't you tell me how awful I look?" I asked, only half-joking. I really did look terrible. My hair was greasy, my face ghostly-pale, and somehow I'd gotten even thinner despite the food tray trying to feed me every hour.

Bastian took my hand in his. I looked at his reflection in the mirror, but he wouldn't meet my gaze. "You're beautiful," he told me. "So beautiful that it hurts sometimes to look at you."

I sucked in a quick breath, too stunned to reply. Then his other hand reached for my waist.

"Dance with me?" he asked, and I looked around.

"But there's no music." I reasoned breathlessly.

Bastian smiled before the soft sound of piano keys broke through the silence, followed by a bow floating across the strings of a violin. I peered around Bastian, seeing that the instruments that had been lifeless moments ago were now playing on their own, breathing life into the place with a haunting melody.

My gaze returned to Bastian, and he began to move with the music, taking a step back and then twirling me with his paw. As I spun, I found that I was laughing. I couldn't remember the last time I'd danced, though I was fairly certain that it had been with my father when I was a child and mother had still been alive.

"You dance so well," I told him breathlessly, the sweeping music moving us across the floor as if we were made of air.

"Despite my appearance," he said as he spun me again, "I'm a very good dancer. The best that gold can buy, in fact. One of the duties of being a prince."

"It wasn't all bad, then," I said, taking his hand back in mine.

"No, not all of it. But," he continued, and I moved closer to him when his paw flexed slightly at my waist, "nothing could've taught me what it would be like to lose my father. Or to become the Beast. Some things you just can never be prepared for."

Thinking of my mother, and my father and sisters, I said, "I know exactly what you mean."

Then the music stopped, and so did we. Standing there, inches apart, a strange kind of current passed between us, and I started to grow lightheaded.

"Come outside with me," Bastian said softly, and I followed him toward one of the other mirrors, hoping fresh air would suffocate the butterflies in my stomach.

It was a strange contrast, the two of us in the reflection. Bastian looked like, well, a beast, and I wasn't much better. Granted, I enjoyed not having as much hair as Bastian did, but the silver veins of my scars seemed to jump out at me from the candlelight. I noticed that Bastian still wouldn't look in the mirror at all.

There was a handle on one of the mirrors that was so small I didn't notice it until Bastian reached out and turned it, bringing me through a door.

Cold winter air enveloped me as we stepped outside onto a stone balcony that reached around the corners of the castle and out of sight. In the distance, I could see the Black Forest, and then the snow-covered hills of the abandoned farm land beyond that. And there, in the blackness of the night sky, was the moon, surrounded by bright, twinkling stars, bathing the world in a soft white.

"I used to come here all the time to look out at Briar—it has the best views in the entire castle," he told me, peering out into the night. "When my father was still the king, I'd climb down the trellises and escape to the barn where the horses were. Brushing their manes calmed me more than anything else would." He looked down. "But when I became the Beast, they were all frightened of me. Except for Hross; she's in the stables now. She's the only one that stuck around after. Besides Sophie, of course."

I wasn't sure what to say. I wanted to feel bad for who Bastian had been in the past, but I wasn't sure I could, knowing the tyrant he would become when he was king. Looking away, I saw that there was an ornate bench that lined the balcony, framed by potted plants that had blooming in them roses of all different shades, even though it was the dead of winter and they were covered in snow. Some of the petals even looked like they were made of glass.

He picked one off its stem—a red one.

"My lady," he said, offering it to me.

"Much obliged, good sir," I said, taking it from him, smiling despite myself.

Bastian sat down and waited for me to take the spot next to him. When I did, I crossed my ankles, regarding him.

"Why didn't you destroy the mirrors in the ballroom?" I asked.

"That was my parent's ballroom," he explained. "Sophie once told me that they used to go in there when they'd ordered most of the staff to retire for the night, and dance alone together. They hadn't had any music, but they didn't need it. Sophie says she'd never seen two people more in love than my parents."

I took his hand and nodded, knowing there was nothing I could really say to fill that void, but I wanted him to know that he wasn't alone. That I could understand some of his pain. My parents had been in love once, I was sure, but I never knew the kind of love that Bastian talked about.

"Right after my mother died," I began, realizing he didn't know much about my past, and yet I felt like I knew more than enough about his, "I used to sleep in her garden to see if she would show up and surprise me. That it had been some grand joke, and she'd come back to us. But I never looked at that garden again once I understood that she was never coming back, and without her there to tend it," I looked away, "her plants withered and died until there was nothing left. I just wish I'd been able to keep it alive for her, you know?"

Bastian put a gentle paw beneath my chin, and I looked up into his eyes. They weren't full of pity like I'd been expecting, but understanding.

"I'm sorry," he told me, "about your mother. I wish I could've met her."

I nodded, steeling myself, and he dropped my chin. "I think she would've liked you," I told him, pausing carefully before I continued. "I had more time with mine than I could've hoped for. I feel awful that you never got to meet yours."

"It never would've been enough time," he told me softly.

I couldn't remember the last time I'd missed my mother this much, but the aching in my heart was almost a comfort now. That I had known that kind of love was more than Bastian had ever had. And there was the love of my sisters' too—besides his governess, Bastian had been alone all this time.

In the comfortable silence, panic and guilt turned my stomach as I thought about how I was going to tell him that I needed to leave him to check on my sisters.

"I have something to confess," he said after a moment before I could speak up. "It's something I'm not proud of, and I would understand if you hated me afterwards."

I straightened, heart in my throat as I waited for him to explain.

He took a deep, trembling breath. "When I realized I couldn't change myself back into the man I'd once been," he began, "I decided to play by the witch's rules and tried to force women to love me."

Knowing there had to be more to it, I clenched my jaw to keep from reacting. "I started venturing out towards town, hoping a girl would wander too far into the Black Forest, and when she did, I would bring her here."

He put his head in his paws, and I found that I was touching his back, comforting him. Even though he'd done a terrible thing, I couldn't think the worst of him yet. That's not the Bastian I knew.

"It was wrong—so terribly, awfully *wrong*—but back then I didn't care," he explained further. "I would've done almost anything to break the curse. But they always ran away at night, trying to get back home, and the wolves…"

Impulsively, I put both my arms around him, imagining those girls who hadn't known the kinds of dangers that the Black Forest held at night.

"How many?" I asked softly when he didn't continue.

Bastian shook his head. "Even one was too many. In the end, the third girl ran off after only a day. That was when I decided I wouldn't ruin the lives of others just because I could. Just because my own life was ruined."

My heart ached painfully, for those girls, for Bastian. This Bastian would've never done something like that, and I could tell how much his past tore him apart now.

"I understand," I told him after he was quiet for a moment.

His head snapped towards me so quickly that he only narrowly missed bumping my forehead.

"That was part of who you used to be, Bastian," I said, lightly touching the fur on his face. "The you I know would never do that."

Bastian looked at me pleadingly. "But what if I'm still that creature? What if, underneath all of this"—he gestured to himself—"I haven't changed at all?"

"You're not that man anymore," I told him resolutely. "I've done things I'm not proud of, especially when I was a child." I specifically remembered cutting off chunks of Emily's hair with my mother's gardening shears because she'd stolen my hair brush. Not that it compared to what Bastian had done, but there wasn't a person alive that hadn't done something they regretted.

"But I grew up," I continued, "and I'm not that person. And neither are you. Our past doesn't define us; it makes us stronger."

Bastian let out a long breath, and I could tell he'd been holding that deep in his heart for a long time. Sophie must've known, but she was loyal enough to Bastian not to say anything.

Like the loyalty I felt towards my sisters. And now, towards Bastian.

"Belle…" he began again after a moment. But he must've seen the distress on my face, and he stopped. "What's wrong?" he asked.

I sighed; he knew me too well. It was as good a time as any. "I have something I need to tell you, too."

He looked at me expectantly.

"Do you know why I've stayed here this long?"

He laughed once and reached out so that his thumb could stroke my palm, distracting me. "Well I'm sure it's not on my account."

"Not exactly," I said. Turning towards him, my hand slipping out of his. "I went out into the Black Forest that night because I was sent to find you."

"By whom?" he asked, curiously tilting his head.

"The Regime."

Bastian pushed his shoulders back. "And why would the Regime have sent you?"

"My father," I explained. "He gambled all of our money away, and then some. He owes the Regime a large debt that he can't pay. He offered me up for the Brothel as payment, but I was able to make another deal." A movement caught my attention, and I noticed Bastian's paws were balled tightly into fists. When I looked back up, his eyes were ablaze with anger.

"Did I say something wrong?" I asked.

He shook his head, and replied in a strained voice, "No, please continue."

"I made a deal with Thomas, the town lawman: that I'd bring back something the Emperor desperately wants as long as he lets my sisters go and forgives my father's debt."

"And what does the Emperor want so desperately, besides my kingdom?" he growled.

I swallowed. "Your ring. The one that cursed you."

"Ha!" he laughed humorlessly. "That thing will do him more harm than good. It would be his downfall were he to possess it." He turned thoughtful. "In fact, I can think of no better punishment for the man trying to steal what's rightfully mine."

I looked away. "It does seem that way, doesn't it?"

He paused before asking, "What aren't you telling me?"

"The other part of the deal." I glanced up at him. "When I return to Briar with the ring, I'll be forced to marry Thomas."

Bastian grabbed my hands, his anger turned to desperation. "Then don't go back."

"But if I don't, he'll kill my father and send both my sisters to the Brothel."

He sat back, dropping my hands from his paws before turning them to fists. "I'll kill him," he growled.

I appreciated the offer, but I'd been dreaming about all the ways I could kill Thomas since that night. "I'd like to do that myself, but I'm not sure how much good it'll do. Bastian, I need to see my sisters. I just need to know that they're alright, that he hasn't done something to them in my absence."

He nodded. "I have a way."

I cocked my head to the side, waiting.

"More magic," he clarified, and I nodded, still not sure what he meant.

We stood and started towards the open door that led back to the ballroom. I wish we didn't have to leave this moment, but we didn't have a choice. The candlelight inside had dimmed so that shadows plagued the mirrors, and I felt a sudden longing for something I would likely never have.

Once we'd left the ballroom, he led me down the corridor to his chambers. The torches lit as we passed them, and Bastian opened his door without a second's hesitation. He immediately went past his bed and flung back the curtain beside it. What I thought might've been a window when I'd first been here was actually a mirror. The only mirror I'd seen in the castle besides the ones in the ballroom. It was tinted the oddest hue of purple.

I came to stand beside him.

"Say one of your sisters' names and the mirror will show her to you," he told me.

I looked at him strangely, but didn't have the patience to question it, so I nodded anyway and spoke clearly. "Emily Fairfax, please."

The purple tint began to swirl across the mirror like the curling smoke from the dark figure Bastian had conjured outside the castle, and behind it an image appeared.

It was my room. I felt like I was seeing it through a window: all my things were exactly where I'd left them, even the vase of flowers I'd put by the window at the end of fall that had become wilted and dried-out. I wondered if this was like the tea visions, a glimpse of something that had happened in the past. But there was Emily on my bed, her hands on her face, her whole body quivering. She was...crying. I moved closer to the mirror, wishing I could reach out to comfort her.

"Emmy," a voice called, and I recognized it as Lila's. "What's wrong?"

My little sister walked into my room, covered in mud, dripping it onto the floor in her wake. If I'd been home, I would've scolded her. But I wasn't.

Emily wiped her hand angrily over her eyes and slid off the bed. "Nothing Lila. Why are you all muddy?"

"I was working in the garden one last time." Her voice was so small... *Wait, one last time?* What had she meant by one last time?

"Come here," Emily said, and Lila bounded into her arms, clutching at my other sister's faded gray tunic.

Tears burned behind my eyes, and I wished more than anything that I could be there with them. I felt Bastian move closer, trying to comfort me.

"Do you think Belle will be back in time?" Lila asked as she buried her face into Emily's stomach.

"Thomas is coming for us in less than a day," Emily said in answer, smoothing Lila's hair down. "I doubt Belle will even know what's happened."

"Less than a day?" I wondered aloud. "That's all they have left is a *day?*"

"You haven't been here more than a week," Bastian observed. "What was your deal with Thomas exactly?"

Without taking my eyes off my sisters, I hurried through a short explanation of the deal, ending with the fact that he'd stipulated the time limit to be a month. He was going against his word; he hadn't been expecting me to come back at all. I wondered if he'd already killed my father.

"Show me Eric Fairfax," I commanded the mirror, and smoke enveloped my sisters before it cleared again to reveal a jail cell. Father was huddled in the corner, dressed in the sooty rags I'd last seen him in, teeth chattering. He had a gash along his jawbone and his parchment-pale skin was dotted with beads of sweat. I put my hand over my mouth, because even though my father only ever cared about himself, and it was probably his own fault that he was in there, he was still my father and I knew he loved us. And we still loved him.

I took in a stilted breath and turned from the mirror. I couldn't look at my father anymore, but I couldn't meet Bastian's eyes either. He stepped towards me, wrapping me in his arms. My hands, which had been clenched into fists, reached around him and clutched at the back of his sweater.

"You must go," Bastian said into my hair.

I pulled back, keeping my arms around his waist. "But what about you?"

He smiled sadly, brushing my cheek with his paw. "Don't worry about me. This is more important." Swallowing hard, he looked away. "Let me get you the ring."

He released me and went over to his desk as emptiness enveloped me. Opening a low drawer, he picked through a few layers of old, crinkled papers before pulling out a wooden box that fit in his palm. It was made of stained dark wood and had strange symbols carved into it. He pulled out a key on a chain hidden beneath his sweater and placed it carefully in the brass lock. There was a click, and he grabbed a pair of black gloves from that same drawer before shutting it, bringing them over to me.

"You must remember never to touch the ring, under any circumstances," he said sternly as he gave me the gloves. I slipped them on and he handed me the box. "Go to the stable behind the castle that I told you about. The forest wolves won't attack if you go quickly on horseback without stopping."

I stopped for a moment, thinking about how I was holding the thing that had cursed Bastian. "I don't want to take the box from you." It was some small excuse, but it was all I had.

Bastian touched it as it lay in my hands. "It will be a reason for you to come back."

I bit my lip, tears stabbing behind my eyes painfully. "I already have a reason." Quickly, I reached up to kiss him on the side of his snout. "Thank you, for letting me save my family."

He looked unbearably sad. "I suppose you owe me again."

Instead of answering, I hurried out the door, forcing myself to focus on getting to my sisters in time, and not how my heart was being torn apart.

I went back through the ballroom and yanked the door open to the outside, the winter air sharpening my senses. I looked over the edge of the stone and saw that I wasn't far from the ground. There was less snow to land on than there was on the other side of the castle, but I had to take my chances; as far as I could tell, this was the closest I was going to get to where Bastian had told me the stables were.

And I was running out of time.

I stepped up onto the stone railing and jumped, bending my knees as my feet hit the ground hard. Pain shuddered up my bad leg, but I ignored it, limping through the discomfort.

Turning the corner towards the back of the castle, I searched the scattered grounds and found the stables easily, its roof covered in dead leaves and fallen pine needles. Slushing through the melting snow to the open structure, I found only one horse—a chestnut-colored mare—but she was beautiful. I grabbed onto her wild black mane and swung up, wishing I could take the time to saddle her. She grunted at me, her breath billowing up like smoke from the cold. But I leaned down and whispered her name into her ear softly, before I dug my riding boots into her sides and she took off into the night.

As I passed the castle, I heard a loud, low howl pierce the night. I told myself it had only been one of the forest wolves.

# CHAPTER 22

## Desert an Unhappy Beast

BASTIAN

I SAT on the edge of my bed, my head in my paws, choosing between utter regret and resolve, knowing that I'd done the right thing by letting her go. I liked to think that Belle wanted to come back. But why would she? She'd gotten what she'd come here for and I'd let her leave with it. She would have her sisters and her father to take care of now.

It was over.

My chest felt empty, and I let the sensation consume me. I wondered at the point now, of living, when I'd come so close to something real. Even if it would've never broken the curse, I'd begun to see myself through her eyes, and for the first time since becoming the Beast, I didn't hate what I was.

I wondered, too, if it would've changed anything had I told her the curse had to be broken before the fifth of February—at the five-year mark—otherwise I'd remain the Beast forever. I'd tried to put it out of my head, but that was only a day away now, and she had to save her family. I knew that, but it didn't make it hurt any less.

With her, I wouldn't have minded staying this way.

But none of that mattered because she wasn't coming back. At least, not in time to save me. If she loved me like I thought she did, I would lose my magic anyway, and then I would die. I wasn't sure the story had mentioned that part, but she would've left to save her sisters regardless.

A knock at the door sounded—I barely heard it.

"Bastian," Sophie called. I didn't have the strength to answer her.

She came in anyway, like she always did. "I heard your howl. What happened?" She looked around. "Where's Belle?"

"Gone," I said lifelessly.

"Gone?"

I hung my head. "Her sisters and father were in danger. I had to let her go to them."

Sophie put her hands on her hips. "But she would've broken the curse. And now that she's left, you're going to waste away and die! How could you let her go?"

I looked at Sophie. "Because I love her. Because she needed to save her family, and she never would've forgiven me for keeping her here while they were in trouble. And I never would've forgiven myself for it either, knowing I'd hurt her."

"Oh, Bastian…" She moved towards me, hands reaching out.

"Please, leave me," I said softly. She looked at me for a moment, her gaze full of sadness and pity, then she left.

I stayed where I was, waiting to die.

# CHAPTER 23

*Let Her Heart Guide Her*

## BELLE

I REACHED the cottage in no time at all. The wolves hadn't attacked me, as Bastian had said, and for that I was grateful. But now, with a winter storm sweeping down from the mountains, I had to face something much worse.

As I got closer, the horse's hooves sloshing through the snow and mud, I saw that there was light coming from the inside. I hoped my sisters were there, still sitting on my bed, holding each other close without any hope that I'd make it back in time. It was better than any of the other fates I was imagining for them.

It had started to sleet now, but the cold never reached me. I tied the mare to a nearby oak tree and ran through the mud to the front door. I flung it open without knocking, and breathed a sigh of relief when the first thing I saw was my sisters huddled by a low fire.

But they weren't alone.

Thomas was there too, along with a few of the Regime soldiers from before, and my heart sank. Everyone except my sisters had their backs turned to me, but the door slammed so loudly against the wall from the wind that six pairs of eyes were quick to find my bedraggled figure.

Emily was the first to speak. "Belle?" she choked out. Lila peeked out from behind one of the officer's legs and tears welled up in her eyes when she saw me. Every bone in my body wanted to go to my sisters and never let them go. But I stayed where I was—I still had Thomas to deal with.

"My, my, this is a surprise," the lawman sneered. I could see that he truly *was* surprised, but it wouldn't last for long. "I didn't expect you to make it back alive."

"I can see that, Thomas," I shot back, "since you're going back on our deal."

"I wouldn't get snappy with me, Belle." He nodded to one of his men, and the soldier pointed a gun at my sisters.

"No!" I stepped forward, but Thomas moved towards me purposefully and shoved my shoulder, making me nearly stumble over my own feet.

"You see," Thomas began, prowling towards me again. "I have all the leverage here, young Belle, and one wrong step could end with the death of the people you love." I took a step backwards, hitting the wall as he pressed up against me. My throat burned from holding back bile. "We wouldn't want that, now would we?"

"Let them go," I begged him. "I have what you want."

His eyes traveled to my chest, where my tunic had come unbuttoned. "Indeed you do."

I gritted my teeth and took the ring out of my pocket. I'd stashed the box by the mare in the hopes that Thomas wouldn't find it. It was the only tie to Bastian that I had left, and I'd be damned if he was going to take that away from me too. Thomas's eyes went from my chest to the ring in my gloved hand, and they widened greedily as he snatched it from me. His own hands were gloved, which was a pity.

"Put your guns down," he told his soldiers with a lazy flick of his hand, and a weight felt like it had been lifted off my shoulders as they followed his orders.

Emily and Lila looked relieved, but then they turned to me and their eyes were questioning.

"Go to my room," I told them as I stripped my hands of the soaking gloves. "I'll meet you there."

Lila smiled and bounded down the hallway, but Emily gave me a knowing, frightened look as she backed away. She knew that I wouldn't be coming to my room to get them. In all likelihood, I would never see them again.

Thomas pocketed the ring and was now staring at me hungrily. "I'm sure you remember the other part of our agreement?"

I swallowed but said nothing. He reached up and touched his finger to my cheek, dragging it down roughly to my neck. Even though it hadn't been the cheek with the scars, I cringed away from him and he laughed.

"All in good time, sweet Belle. Your mother never wanted me, but by tomorrow, you'll be mine. Guards." He motioned to his men and two of them came up to me, each taking an arm. I didn't struggle—I knew that if I did anything against Thomas, he'd take it out on my sisters.

But then, Thomas went into the back of the house, and I heard my sisters scream as he pulled them from my room and hauled them back into the living room.

"What are you doing?" I demanded. "Leave them alone, I've done as you asked!"

He grinned awfully. "I'm taking them to the Brothel, of course."

I shook with anger and betrayal. "That was *not* part of our deal, Thomas." But he ignored me. He tore one of Emily's sleeves to expose part of her shoulder as she struggled against his hold. She was near tears; Lila was already bawling.

"They're only children! Please, let them go—I'll do anything."

"I like anything," he replied. He let Lila go and she slumped to the ground, but he kept Emily in his grasp. "I haven't followed our deal very closely up to now, so why would you think I'd show you any mercy by suddenly being a man of my word? Besides, getting the ring was only part of my agreement with the Emperor." He came closer to me. "The other, more delicious, part is that if I find the Beast and kill it, I'll become his second in command."

I gasped, and my nails bit hard into my palms. *No, not Bastian.*

"So, you see," he continued, "it's really quite convenient that you *did* come back, so that, now, you can lead the way."

"Never." I struggled against the guards. "I'll never show you where he is."

Thomas raised an eyebrow. "Not even for your sisters?"

I hesitated, torn between my sisters—my family—and the man that I'd come to care for so deeply I missed him even now. It shouldn't have even been a choice, but I wasn't sure I could stand being the reason that Bastian died.

Thomas laughed cruelly. "Well, well, this is quite a turn of events. Are you telling me that you feel something for the Beast?"

I didn't answer, knowing I was damned no matter what I said.

Thomas' eye twitched and heat spread up his neck. "I can't believe you actually care for that monstrous creature. Listen, Belle Fairfax, you belong to me," he said, infuriated but resolute. "Now I have all the more reason to kill the Beast."

I remained defiant. "You'll never be able to find the castle."

"Oh, I have a way. I was just hoping you'd be more cooperative, but I can see you're a lost cause." One of the guards stepped forward as Thomas motioned to him.

"This is Jean-Luc," Thomas explained. "Among his many other talents, he's an excellent tracker. So good, in fact, that he had no trouble keeping up with you that night I sent you out into the Black Forest. He told me all about your encounter with the wolves—how the Beast saved your life. How the creature was so distraught from the state of you that he didn't even notice Jean-Luc nearby."

My heart stopped. "No."

"Oh, yes," he sneered.

I struggled against the guard's grasps, but their hold was like iron. I couldn't breathe. How could I stop them from killing Bastian? I thought to stall, but what good would that do?

"Why didn't you just come find me when I'd first made it to the castle and kill him then?" I asked anyway.

Thomas looked at me like I was an idiot. "Because if I'd killed the Beast before you'd gotten the ring from him, we likely would've never found it. No, it was easier this way."

My heart ached. I'd known Thomas was using me, but not like this.

"So, what is the Beast worth to you?" Thomas continued, grasping the hilt of a dagger that sat in the scabbard around his belt.

My sisters were now huddled in a corner together, but he paid them no attention. I hoped he'd forget them, and with any luck, they'd still have father when all this was over. But I couldn't let him kill Bastian.

"My life," I answered in a near-whisper, and his hand froze on the dagger.

"No!" Emily cried out, and one of the soldiers moved in to silence her, putting a hand over her mouth and muffling her outcry. I heard Lila start to whimper as I stared Thomas down.

"You would die for that thing—that *monster*?" Thomas asked incredulously.

I shook my head. "He's not a monster, Thomas. *You* are."

Thomas stormed up to me, and the guards held me up so that we were eye to eye, their tight grip on my arms making them numb. Thomas now held the blade of his dagger close to my face, his eyes aflame. Then he dragged it hard down the side of my face with the silver scars and I couldn't help the cry of pain that escaped me.

When he was finished carving into my skin, ending at my jawline, Thomas looked at the blade in morbid curiosity as he spoke, "A monster is all he'll be once I put this through his heart."

Tears streamed down my face, unbidden. "Please, don't."

Thomas laughed humorlessly and straightened. "Don't you realize that the more you try to protect the Beast, the less chance either of you has of making it through the night? Your affection for him is turning what would've been a mercy killing into a slow and painful death."

I clenched my jaw to keep from saying anything else.

"I'm glad you finally understand the situation you're in," he said to my silence. "I've already sent some of my men to the castle. They should be breaking down the door any moment."

He motioned towards the front of the cottage, and the soldiers tightened their grip on my arms and forced me outside. The wind had grown colder and the sleet was coming down harder. I was soaked in minutes, but I barely felt it. I had to figure out a way to keep them from killing Bastian. This was all my fault; I *had* to fix it.

Even if it killed me.

One of the Guards pressed my wrists together in front of me and clamped them down with handcuffs; they were too tight on my skin, but the pain of it was numb in the cold. The same Guard lifted me up onto the back of his horse, and then saddled up behind me.

"Where are you taking me?" I yelled to Thomas.

"The castle, of course," he explained.

"Why?"

Thomas's eyes darkened. "So that you can watch the life leave your precious Beast."

I was about to protest when the Guard behind me tied a cloth around my mouth as a gag. I screamed against it until my voice was hoarse, but it was pointless. Thomas watched me struggle in vain with an odd glint in his eye. My gaze pleaded with the lawman, searching for the part of him that was still human.

He ignored me, turning his horse to face the way of the castle.

~

The sleet was relentless as we started towards the Black Forest. The gag had already grown soggy in my mouth and my head bobbed forward with exhaustion. The protective clothing that the Regime soldier behind me had on was unyielding and every one of my muscles was sore. But that didn't stop me from trying to find a way to get to Bastian before Thomas. We weren't trotting, but we certainly weren't galloping either, and, as Thomas had said, some of his men were already there. He must've had the confidence that they were somehow keeping Bastian detained. But they hadn't seen him take down a wolf like I had. At least it wouldn't be easy, and that would buy me some time.

I slumped forward further, working out a plan quickly in my head. The Regime soldier slowed his horse, leaning slightly forward to check on me like I'd hoped he would, and I snapped my head back. There was a sharp crack and then a thump behind me. My head swam from the pain, but I grabbed onto the loose reigns carefully with my shackled hands and stopped the horse. He snorted his annoyance at me as I slid down his back.

I stumbled and fell to the wet ground awkwardly, starting to sink into the mud of the forest. But I righted myself quickly, hurrying toward where the Regime soldier had fallen to see that blood spattered his nose and lip;

he was out cold.

Searching his pockets for the key, I felt the cold metal of it between my fingers in his jacket, and placed the key in my mouth as I turned it in the lock. The metal released and clanged to the wet ground, and I hissed at the stinging on my wrists. I'd moved around in them too much, and I saw where layers of skin had started to chafe off in red, angry marks. I held my hands to my chest for a moment, gritting my teeth, before pushing the discomfort out of my head. There was nothing I could do about it now.

Fighting against the cutting sensation of the freezing rain, I unhooked the soldier's rifle from his belt, grabbed as many bullets as I could carry from his jacket pocket, and started towards the edge of the Black Forest.

I'd never shot a rifle before, but I knew the basics from reading about them. I checked the chamber to see if there was already a bullet there, placing the rest of them in my pocket. I swallowed hard at the idea of shooting anyone. It felt different than shooting someone with an arrow somehow, more personal. And I'd only ever killed animals with my bow, anyway. I shook my head to dispel the thought—I'd do whatever it took to save Bastian, even if that meant killing some of the people that were after him. They wouldn't hesitate to do the same to me.

Unshed tears burned behind my eyes as I imagined the worst: that Bastian was already gone, dying with the thought that I'd led the soldiers there. The guilt tore at me and I moved faster.

Suddenly, I heard someone swear behind me. I turned to see Thomas pointing his gun at my head, sitting atop his horse.

"Crafty girl," he said, though not as if he was impressed. Irritation and anger had disfigured his face. "I knew I should've watched you myself. Drop the gun, Belle. Let's not make this any more difficult than it has to be."

I was barely paying attention to him, though, as I caught the movement of a shadow flitting in the trees behind Thomas. I heard him cock his rifle. "I said—"

But he didn't get to repeat himself as I watched Bastian come charging out of the darkness of the Black Forest.

# CHAPTER 24

*Fear Nothing*

<u>BASTIAN</u>

**M**Y ONLY thoughts were of Belle. The way she'd smiled at me, the way she'd touched me without even realizing she was doing it. I imagined over and over in my head how she would've finally told me that she loved me. I wanted to live the rest of my life hearing her say those words, had seen it play out in my head like a fairytale. But all I'd had with her was a week.

I'd never imagined this could happen; that I'd find the girl to break the curse, and then she'd have to leave me. And that I'd let her go. But I'd brought this curse upon myself and now I had to live with the consequences—I could never blame Belle for taking back her freedom to save her family.

I found I couldn't keep myself from wanting to see her, though, despite the pain I knew it would cause.

I knelt in front of the magic mirror, and told it, with stilted breath, "Show me Belle."

The mirror swirled, and I expected to see Belle hugging her sisters, perhaps her father too, tucked safely away in their cottage now that the cursed ring was with the awful lawman and on its way to the Emperor. At least I would die knowing that she was happy.

But what I saw when the smoke cleared turned my blood cold.

Belle was being held against the wall of her cottage by two Regime soldiers, and another man not dressed in uniform was very close to her, trailing a dagger down her cheek. Red blood popped up where her skin was being torn open, and an unchecked anger rose up in me when she screamed. My claws slashed out, and the mirror shattered beneath them.

Then, there was a loud banging against the castle doors, echoing all the way back to my chambers, and I flinched. Sophie rushed in, appearing frazzled. "There's an army of Regime soldiers trying to break into the castle!"

Leaving the shattered remains of my mirror, I told her, "Get somewhere safe. I don't want them to find you."

"What about you?" she practically yelled.

"I'll take care of them."

She grabbed my arm. "No, Bastian, I won't let you do this alone."

I looked down at her. "You're the only mother I've ever had. You loved me even *before* I became the Beast, when I was the real monster. Don't make me watch you get hurt because of me."

Because I knew why they were here: they'd found my castle and they were going to kill me and take my throne. But I had to get to Belle as soon as possible, and that might mean fighting my way through the soldiers at my door, and any others that got in my way.

She set her jaw and I knew she wouldn't budge from the issue, so I took her by the arm and gently pushed her into the nearest closet, closing it swiftly and locking her inside.

She pounded at the wood. "Bastian!"

"It's for your own good, Soph," I said through the door.

I heard a much louder bang than before and then the splintering of wood.

I realized I couldn't take on however many soldiers they'd sent. Besides, killing a wolf was one thing, but killing a human made me a different kind of beast. I quickly cast a spell that would enchant every item in the castle to come to life and fight against the soldiers, but I knew that would only buy me a few minutes.

The spell I casted drained my magic, but my anger at the man who'd hurt Belle gave me the strength to stumble from my chambers, through the ballroom, and out the back way. Sophie was safe, and now the only thing that mattered was Belle.

# CHAPTER 25

## I Would Die To Save Him from Pain

<u>BELLE</u>

*BASTIAN!* I called out to him in my head, but he only had eyes for Thomas.

Thomas followed my gaze, and I saw him start to swing his rifle around. But Bastian was too fast, and he pounced on Thomas, tearing him from his horse and tackling him to the ground. The horse reared up for a moment, its hooves pawing at the air, then it shot off towards town.

I turned back to see Bastian and Thomas struggle for a moment, the soldier's rifle held loosely in my hands, knowing that I could hit Bastian if I tried to shoot Thomas. They were tumbling through the mud, and it was obvious that Bastian had the upper hand; Thomas was using his rifle lengthwise to keep away Bastian's sharp fangs, but it wouldn't be long until—

A bullet sliced through the air and flew into Bastian's shoulder; he reared back. Swinging around, I looked out into the forest to see where it had come from, and saw half a dozen Regime soldiers heading towards us from town.

"No," Thomas managed to yell. "The Beast is mine!"

The soldiers stopped their assault, looking thrown for a moment, their rifles still trained on Bastian. I wasn't sure if they'd seen me yet or not, but I dropped to the ground, landing softly in the mud with my rifle pointed at the soldiers. As they cocked their weapons, I yelled, "Bastian, look out!"

Bastian turned towards my voice, his eyes full of the same relief and concern that I felt in my heart. But Thomas took advantage of our exchange, and I couldn't get the words out before he hit Bastian in the jaw with the butt of his rifle.

I locked my jaw and took aim at the soldiers with the deadly machine in my hands, hoping my skills in archery would be of some help to me. I placed my finger near the trigger before taking a breath and opening fire.

I aimed the bullet at the trees first, giving them a warning shot and making them scatter behind the large trunks of the Black Forest—I really didn't want to have to kill anyone, and the force behind the shot frightened me a little. I heard Bastian and Thomas still struggling a few yards away from me as I dug another bullet out of my pocket, and realized that death couldn't be avoided. One of them was going to die tonight, but it wouldn't be Bastian if I had anything to do with it.

The soldiers began shooting towards me, and I went to put my finger on the trigger to fire back, but then a knee dig into my back before I could. I cried out in surprise, and the person pinning me down grabbed my arms and cuffed them behind my back before turning me over. It was the soldier who I'd been riding with that I'd knocked out, the blood from his nose still splattered across his face. He slapped me across my split cheek hard before pulling me up to stand.

"Lawman Thomas," he barked out, "I have the girl."

I stopped breathing—where did I know that voice from?

I craned my neck to look back at the soldier, who hadn't seemed any different from the others, and my heart stopped. *No.*

"Sean?"

His gaze flicked to me for a moment, then back to Thomas.

"What's happened to you—what have they *done*?" I asked him. Sean still looked the same, though his brown hair was shorter and his normally piercing green eyes were dulled.

"The inevitable," he told me, keeping his gaze on Bastian and Thomas, who had now stopped fighting. I glanced at Bastian, and his eyes were wide in panic; Thomas was sneering in triumph.

"What did they do to you?" I asked when I'd turned back to him, horrified.

He smiled coldly. "Nothing I didn't want them to do. I'm new again. Better than I was before. The man who baked bread in his father's bakery and wanted to make you his wife is gone now, and in his place is the perfect soldier."

I heard Bastian growl, but ignored him.

"But what about your father?" I asked, fearing I already knew the answer.

That made his jaw tick, though his voice remained calm. "Dead."

I let out a shaky breath. "Dead? But how?"

"We were raided by Regime soldiers a couple nights ago," he told me. "Apparently, my father had been keeping some of the Regime coin for himself. He deserved everything the Regime did to him." Horror and disgust filled my stomach, making me want to throw up. I couldn't believe what I was hearing: the Sean I'd known had loved his father more than anything.

"After they killed him," he continued, "Thomas gave me a choice: die with him, or join the Regime. I chose the better option—the *only* option."

"The only option" I told him coldly, "was death."

He shrugged his shoulders. "That's your opinion. One that'll get you killed, but I suppose you're entitled to it." Then he called out to Thomas again, "Where should I take her, sir."

Thomas smiled wickedly, his rifle now trained on Bastian. "Take her back to the Fairfax's cottage. I have plans for them both before the night is over."

Sean nodded in obedience, then dragged me back towards home, the gun still loosely pointed at my head as I watched the other Regime soldiers come out from behind the trees. Their guns remained pointed at Bastian until they'd secured him. I tried to catch his eye, hoping that he could see that I wanted him to break their hold on him and go back to his castle where he would be safe. But when he met my gaze, his was fierce and determined, and I knew he wouldn't leave me, no matter how much I wanted him to.

I hung my head as Sean pulled me along, and I wondered hopelessly how were we going to get out of this.

# CHAPTER 26

*Cruel One*

<u>BASTIAN</u>

THE HANDCUFFS bit into my wrists, tearing at the fur there and pulling my skin. I thought again about how I was going to break these bonds and go after the town lawman, Thomas. The man who'd taken Belle's sisters from her, the man who'd hurt Belle in so many ways that I wished I could tear off a limb for each one, and who was brandishing a blood-soaked dagger at me now.

But if I challenged him, he'd hurt Belle. And I couldn't allow that. I'd last as long as I could, hoping she'd find a way out before he killed me.

The weight of my own head was finally too much, and my chin rested blissfully on my torn chest. I could feel my blood running down to the floor in slow drips from where he'd cut me. But I couldn't feel the pain anymore.

"You're a poor excuse for a beast," Thomas told me, and when I remained silent, he swung out with the dagger and cut across my cheek. I barely flinched.

"I can't believe you actually think she loves you," he continued. "It was all for the ring, you know. She was doing *my* bidding, so that she and I could be wed and want for nothing under the care of the Emperor himself."

Thomas crouched down so that I was forced to look him in the eye. "How could someone, even with all the…flaws she has, love a Beast?"

At that, my head snapped up, and I growled, straining against my restraints as I bared my teeth at him. The only flaws he could be talking about were her scars, and I loved them. Every single one of them.

Thomas flinched away from me and tried to hide the fear I saw in his eyes by turning away for a moment, as if lost in thought. I felt myself smiling at the small triumph, until bone-deep exhaustion overtook me again. My power was draining with each passing moment, bringing me closer to death. I wondered idly if Thomas knew that I was going to die from the curse and he was keeping me alive to suffer through it, or if he simply enjoyed torturing me.

"When Belle and I go to live with the Emperor," he went on, turning back to me now that he'd composed himself, "she'll never want for anything." He gave me an almost-pleading look, which was so uncharacteristic of what I knew of him that I barely heard his next words. "I can give her a normal life. Don't you want that? If you truly love her, shouldn't you want the best for her?"

My blood boiled in my weakened body. He was right, but for all the wrong reasons.

"You can't give her that happiness," I croaked out, tasting iron in my mouth. "She may not love me as I wished she did, but I love her and her *flaws*, as you called them. You only love the idea of what you want her to be—of what you think you can mold her into. But Belle is too strong to be changed by someone like you."

I'd been so focused on my own words that I hadn't noticed Thomas' entire demeanor change. Without warning, his grip tightened on the dagger and he stabbed forward into my left shoulder. The blade went through my flesh like butter until the tip of it hit the bone jarringly. I let out an inhuman howl when he pulled it out of me, and my body strained against the cuffs as I slumped forward.

"You weren't able to best me," Thomas said, wiping off the blade unceremoniously on his pantleg.

I tried to keep my blurred gaze on him, if only to remain conscious. The more time he spent torturing me, the better chance Belle had of escaping.

"And you're at my mercy," he continued. "So, I have to wonder why you haven't begged for your life yet."

Gritting my teeth against the pain, I tried to put venom behind my words. "I'll die before begging you for a *thing*."

Thomas smiled wickedly. "That can be arranged."

# CHAPTER 27

*Loves You Dearly*

BELLE

N O MATTER how awful father had been to us, I'd never wanted out of my home so much before in my life as I did now.

The soldiers had forced Bastian to his knees in the middle of the living room before unceremoniously tossing me into my room and blocking the door. I'd tried to kick it down a couple times, but it was no use—it wouldn't budge.

Now, I sat on my lumpy bed, wringing my captured hands behind my back. I knew I'd pay for the movement later—if there even *was* a later—but I couldn't help it. I needed a plan, and soon.

I knew how to escape my room, of course; trying to kick down my door had just been the easiest way. When father would come home drunk and angry, looking for any living soul to scream his problems at, I used to lift up the floorboards near the window that had always been a bit loose, and make my way through a shallow crawl space to Emily and Lila's room. I'd stayed there all night, not daring to sleep in case father came in looking for them, and then he'd have to answer to me.

But first, I needed to get these cuffs off. If I was going to have a chance to take out the soldiers at my door, my hands would have to be free. And my only plan wasn't great.

I eyed the drawer of my nightstand where I'd always kept a dagger. I hoped that my sisters hadn't moved anything while I'd been gone, but maybe they'd only been in my room the one time.

Seeing my sisters in the mirror—having to leave Bastian so suddenly— seemed like so long ago.

Shaking my head to dispel the memory, I moved across the bed sheets towards the drawer and crouched to reach the handle, the brass filigree cold in my grasp. Thankfully, it opened without a sound, and there was the dagger, glinting softly in the lamplight.

Now was going to be the tricky part.

Picking it up by the leather hilt, I placed it carefully between the bed frame and the inside of the nightstand. It dangled there between the wood for a moment before dropping to the rug below. Sighing, I tried a couple more times before it fit. Once it did, I hurried to the other side of the nightstand and pushed the heavy piece of furniture towards the bed. When I didn't hear the knife fall, I went back to see how stable the hilt was. It didn't budge when I touched it, but it wouldn't hold for very long. I had to make this count.

Carefully placing the blade between one of the thin links in the cuffs,

I started to move my hands up and down, sawing at the metal. It made a quiet grating sound, but I kept my eyes trained on the door, and no one came to stop me. The only sounds I could hear were my own, and the far-off, indecipherable boom of Thomas' voice.

What was likely minutes later, but felt like hours, I heard the metal link snap. I almost cried with relief. It would be a while until I could get the actual cuffs off my wrists, but at least I could move them freely now. The idea of taking a swing at Thomas was very tempting.

*Focus.* I had to rescue Bastian first, and then try to find out where they'd taken my sisters—every second counted.

I hurried over to the loose floorboard, my body aching from what I'd just done, and lifted the wood without a sound.

Lowering myself into the shallow crawlspace feet-first, the fit was much tighter than I remembered. I crept to my sisters' room through mold and mud, turning myself around before lifting the second set of loose floorboards and climbing out. I had a ridiculous thought that I'd have to clean up all the mud I'd just tracked onto the floor, then moved noiselessly to the door, pressing my ear to it. It didn't sound like anyone was outside it, though I still couldn't hear what was being spoken.

Then, I heard a wounded roar. *Bastian.* Tears burned behind my eyes, the idea of Bastian in pain making me feel as if my stomach had been sliced open.

Looking around the room quickly, I searched for something—anything—I could use to knock out the guards that were keeping watch at my door down the hall. I kicked myself for leaving the dagger in my room, but I wasn't sure I had the resolve to stab someone in cold blood anyway.

It didn't take long for my gaze to land on something I knew didn't belong there: mother's frying pan.

*What the hell is the frying pan doing here?* I thought, trying to imagine what my sisters would've been doing with it in their room instead of in the kitchen, and failing. But it didn't really matter why; all that mattered was that it was as good a weapon as I was going to get.

I picked it up gingerly, feeling its weight in my hand, wincing when a chipped part of the rusted handle cut into my skin, and reached for the doorknob. The old metal hinges creaked as the door opened only an inch or two, and I gritted my teeth, hoping it had gone unnoticed. Putting my eye up to the crack I'd made, I had the perfect view of the soldiers. Or, just the one soldier. I wasn't sure what had happened to the second and third man, but I wasn't going to question it.

"Why won't you beg for your life?" I heard Thomas demand, his voice much clearer now.

The guard had his back to my door, but he was looking towards the living room and paying little attention to anything else. Anger flared up inside me—someone just trying to get a look at the Beast, the monster that lived in the forgotten castle.

Luckily, Thomas's voice was drowning out my footfalls while I crept up behind the soldier.

"Fight me!" he demanded, followed by a thud and a low grunt that sounded like it had come from Bastian. Thomas was growing impatient, and I was running out of time.

Just as I came up behind the guard, I heard Thomas ask, "Would things be different if Belle were here to witness your cowardice? Would you fight me then?"

Bastian didn't answer, and I wondered if that was because he chose not to, or because couldn't. Clenching my jaw, I brought the frying pan up and bashed the soldier in the temple with the handle. He crumpled immediately without a sound, and I braced myself under him to break his fall. I didn't care if it hurt him, but it would make too much noise. I let him slide to the floor, grabbed his rifle, and peeked around the corner.

Bastian was being held up by handcuffs that had been nailed against the far wall. His sweater was torn and the fur beneath was matted with blood. Head bowed, I could see that there was more blood speckled in his blond mane. Then Thomas came into view. He had the dagger he'd cut me with in his hand, and the silver and fresh blood gleamed eerily in the firelight.

I trained the rifle on him, my finger twitching against the trigger, and stepped into the room. "Drop it, Thomas."

The lawman flinched, but chuckled darkly as he turned, still holding the dagger, pointing it at me now.

"My, we are resourceful, aren't we? I should stop underestimating you, Belle," he chided, and I brought the rifle up to my eye level.

"I said, drop it!"

I'd shoot him if it came to that, though I was desperately hoping he'd run away like the coward I knew he was.

But I could see in his eyes that his pride and thirst for power was winning out against any cowardice. Gaining the Emperor's favor was everything to him, even more than marrying me.

"Look, Beast," Thomas called, though his angry gaze stayed on me. "Your knight in shining armor is here to save you."

Out of the corner of my eye, I saw Bastian's head raise up painfully, and risked a glance at him. His eyes were lifeless, and I could see the utter defeat in them—until they found me, and widened with fear.

I took a step closer. "I *will* shoot you if you don't drop the dagger," I warned.

Thomas laughed fully now. "I don't think so, Belle. You don't have it in you. Despite what you did to keep your sisters alive all those months without your father, you could never bring yourself to kill me, or any person for that matter."

I breathed in sharply. How had he known about my hunting? My finger twitched against the trigger again, but I steadied it. It didn't matter how he knew, he was right—I didn't have it in me to kill him. Still, I couldn't figure out a way this would end without one of us, or even both of us, ending up dead.

"You're *not* human, Thomas," I said between my teeth.

He narrowed his beady eyes at me, and I could see that I'd let him get closer, the distance between him and Bastian growing. I moved into the room more, putting space between us by escaping towards the kitchen.

Thomas followed my every move, clearly angry from my comment. "Can't you see him for what he is?" he demanded. "Can't you see he's a monster? An ugly, terrible beast? Just look at him!"

I couldn't get distracted again, so I kept my eyes on Thomas. "The only monster here is you. Now put the knife down, before you make me test your theory of whether or not I have the nerve to shoot you."

Thomas swallowed and I actually saw a trace of fear in his eyes. "Fine," he said coldly, placing the knife down on the ground slowly. The rifle in my hands followed him until he stood back up.

"Kick it away," I commanded, and he hesitated before doing as I said. It skittered across the floor and hit the wall by the fireplace with a loud clank.

My arms suddenly felt boneless, and my grip on the gun loosened. I ran over to Bastian as I slung the gun over my shoulder by the strap and touched the bleeding gashes on his face. His blue eyes regarded me with a mixture of wonder and exhaustion.

"I'm so sorry Bastian," I said, tearing away some of what was left of his sweater to see the extent of the damage. I breathed out quickly—it wasn't as bad as I'd first thought, but there were still long, garish slashes across his chest from the dagger, and a part of his shoulder that had been stabbed through to the bone. "You're fine, love. You'll be fine. All we have to do is get you bandaged up and—"

"Belle," Bastian croaked and I looked up at his panicked gaze.

I didn't realize it was a warning until the weight of the rifle was no longer on my back and an arm had reached around my throat, pulling me backwards. I watched as Bastian thrashed uselessly against the tight bindings. I wanted to call out to him to stop—he was just hurting himself more—but I could barely breathe.

"You really thought I'd give up that easily?" Thomas hissed into my ear. He didn't expect an answer, and continued, though more loudly now. "You belong to me!"

My hands clawed at his forearm, but it was useless. He did nothing to stop me from scratching away at his arm, the blood dripping to the floor, and I felt his skin underneath my fingernails. When he'd had enough, he spun me to face him and gripped my face hard with his other hand.

"That *beast* is the only thing standing in the way of everything I've ever wanted, and nothing, not even you, can stop me," he growled, then his eyes softened a bit. "You could learn to love me, you know? We could live comfortably under the Emperor's care. And I'd be able to look past your scars."

I couldn't tell him how wrong he was—that I'd never love him, not if I had a thousand lifetimes. I needed someone that wouldn't just look past my scars, but love them as a part of who I was. So I did the only thing I could and spit in his face. It landed near his eye, but he didn't wipe it away. He actually looked disappointed for a moment before the anger took over and distorted his features.

"Fine, have it your way," he threw me to the side and I landed hard against the floor.

Everything from that point on went too quickly. Ignoring the pain in my hands and knees, I turned to see Thomas bring up the rifle. Scrambling against the blood-slick floor, I ran at him as he placed the rifle at his eye-level, pointing it straight at Bastian. Just as he pulled the trigger, I flew into him. The air was knocked out of me as we crashed to the floor, and Thomas's head cracked against the stone sickeningly.

He didn't move beneath me.

My ears were ringing from the gunshot, but I couldn't make another mistake, not like I had before. I checked Thomas' neck for a pulse. Nothing...

*Bastian.*

I ripped Thomas' keys off his belt with shaking hands, and ran over to Bastian. His breathing was labored and I refused to look at the bloom of red spreading across the lower half of his ribcage. With shaking hands, I managed to get the key into the lock and release him from the cuffs. He slumped down, but I held him up and positioned him so that I could lay him carefully on the ground.

His eyes were closed, his skin frozen underneath the blood-soaked fur. I choked back a sob. "No, no, no," I pleaded. *This is all my fault.* I touched his cheek, and his eyes fluttered open, finding mine. "Stay with me, Bastian."

"Belle," he choked out. His chest was heaving, as if it pained him to take each breath.

"I'm here," I whispered, loosely grasping at the fur on his chest. "I'm right here."

"You're here," he repeated my words, as if he didn't believe it even when it was coming from his own mouth.

Any words I might've said got caught in my throat. Blood pooled from beneath his body where he'd been shot, and my stomach roiled at what it would mean if he lost any more of it.

"I didn't think I'd get to—to see you again before…"

"Stop that," I begged him, stroking his mane. "Can't you heal yourself?"

He cracked a weak smile. "The magic doesn't work like that, Belle. At least, not anymore." Then the smile slipped from his face and turned into a pained grimace.

I moved as close to him as I possibly could. "This is all my fault," I said. "If I hadn't left—if I'd just *stayed* with you—this never would've happened."

"Don't you dare blame yourself," he told me. He brought his paw to my face; it was so cold. "Promise me. Promise me you won't blame yourself, not for a single moment."

I shook my head, but seeing the desperation in his eyes, I told him softly, "I promise." I held his hand to my face, my eyes pleading with him not to let go.

"I love you," he managed, his voice barely a whisper. "Even in death, I will always love you." Then his eyes rolled back and his head lolled to the side.

"No," I whispered, letting his lifeless hand fall to his side. "No, no, Bastian. Please. *Please*, come back." I grabbed his face in my hands. "Come back to me." My eyes searched his face, but it was unmoving.

And then I told him, from the deepest part of my soul: "I love you."

He didn't stir.

I couldn't breathe—my lungs felt trapped in my body. I buried my face in his chest, tears burning, cutting down my cheeks, and something in me broke. *My fault, all my fault that he's dead.* I'd been too late and now he was gone, just as I'd feared. If I'd just stowed my fear earlier, or come up with a quicker plan, or watched my back with Thomas, he might still be alive.

But Bastian was gone and he was never coming back. And it was my doing. My heart tore itself apart at the thought, and a sob ripped from my chest.

The cottage had grown horribly silent—my cries cut through it like a banshee in the night.

Then, a strange light pierced my eyelids, and I opened them to see that the same purple smoke had begun to pour out from the bullet wound in Bastian's chest.

I stood as I wiped at the tears on my face. *Is this what happens after someone with Bastian's curse dies?* I wondered. Not wanting to interfere, I backed away, hoping that he was going somewhere good—somewhere he could be at peace. But he still didn't move, and soon his body was so engulfed by the plumes of odorless smoke that I couldn't see him anymore. And then, the smoke collapsed in on itself, as if it had been sucked back into Bastian's body.

But it wasn't the Beast that laid there now.

It was a man—no fur, no scars except for a map of silver ones. His sweater was hanging on by a few threads, and he was wearing what looked like Bastian's pants, but they were too big on him and rode low on his hips. His eyes were still closed as he lay there, and I wondered who he was and how he'd gotten here. But then he stirred, and I had a sudden irrational hope that maybe it was Bastian—that he'd come back to me.

It couldn't be, though. I'd seen the life leave his eyes. And he'd never looked this human before. This couldn't be Bastian.

The man, who had dirty-blonde hair that went to the nape of his neck, opened his eyes and sat up slowly, holding his hands in front of him and staring at them as if he'd never seen them before. His jaw was angular, his nose sloping and flawless. He had long lean muscles that contracted as he bent his knees and stood effortlessly, looking down at himself as if he didn't believe what he was seeing, his chest and stomach heaving. He reminded me a little of the Bastian I'd seen in the rose-tea visions I'd had in the castle, and I was sure that my mind was playing tricks on me.

Every bone in my body ached for it to be Bastian…but if it wasn't, I didn't have the strength to deal with him.

"Who are you?" I demanded, my voice shaking uncontrollably.

The man's gaze snapped up to meet mine. The way he'd turned to look at himself and the angle of his body made it difficult to see his face at first, but I could tell that he was looking at me.

"Belle?" he asked, and I started at the sound of my name on his lips. It was like the shadow of a voice I'd once known.

"Who are you?" I asked again, more forcefully this time, my heart beating loudly in my chest.

The man approached me slowly. "It's me," he said. "Belle. It's *me.*"

*He couldn't mean*—I didn't dare hope…

The man took another step towards me and his face came into the light, only inches from me now. The silver scars on his jawline stood out against his skin, but otherwise it was unblemished. His dark blond hair was slicked back, and I reached out and took a strand of it between my fingers. It was soft and separated easily.

Then I looked into his eyes and…they were unmistakably *his.*

"Bastian?" I managed.

He smiled as he reached for me, and I caught a glimpse of his perfect teeth before he took me into his arms. Fresh tears cut down my cheeks as I gripped him tight. Not having the cushion of the fur, his body seemed harder—more real, but less real at the same time.

Pulling back, he placed a very human hand on my waist, reaching up with his other hand and touching my cheek, pushing back my wet, knotted hair. I wanted to close my eyes at the sensation, but if I did, this might all be a dream—a dream that I never wanted to wake up from. My gaze strayed to what were now his full lips and back to his eyes.

He was so beautiful it hurt.

A small part of me wondered if this was some sort of trick. If it was, it was cruel and would shatter my heart. But a much bigger part told me this was real. That Bastian was alive—was *human* again.

He pulled me closer and placed his forehead against mine. I sucked in a breath at his closeness, the warmth of his body, and finally closed my eyes, feeling safe for the first time in a long time. I tilted my head back so that our noses brushed and I heard his own breath hitch. My mind was still reeling when he dipped his head down and our lips met.

His were soft and warm, melding effortlessly to mine and stealing my breath. Heat spread through my body as I pressed myself to him and his grip tightened around me. His hands tangled themselves gently in my hair and I gripped the hard muscle of his back, pressing my fingers into his skin.

My hands found their way to his chest, where I brushed his hot skin, traveling up past his neck and into his hair. I grasped the wet tendrils and brought him closer to me. A low sound escaped his throat and his hands skimmed down to my waist, anchoring me to him, deepening the kiss. I was so unbearably lightheaded—I'd never felt anything like this before.

Like I was floating and the only thing anchoring me to the earth was him.

He broke away first, breathing hard against my lips. My eyes opened and found his. They were so bright I could've sworn they truly were made of sapphire.

"I can't believe it's you," I said, but he only smiled as he stroked the hair near my temple languidly.

"I love you," I whispered to him, in case he hadn't heard me the first time, when I thought he'd been dead.

His hand stopped and he smiled. "I know," he said. His voice was still deep, but not nearly what it had been when he was the Beast. I almost missed it. "Otherwise I wouldn't be here. You brought me back to life; you broke my curse." He kissed me once, his lips lingering against mine. "I love you, Belle."

I grinned now. "I know."

He laughed for a moment, and then his eyes went back to my lips. We were so close, I could barely breathe…

Then I remembered my sisters.

I wrenched away from him without meaning to, and something twisted in my gut at the hurt that flashed across his face.

"My sisters," I explained, and I knew he understood when his face grew concerned. "We have to hurry."

I looked at him again for a moment, still not quite believing my own eyes, when I realized that he was practically half-naked and in desperate need of clothes. Heat shot up my neck to my cheeks when I saw that he was watching my gaze linger on him.

Clearing my throat, I said, "Let me get you some of my father's clothes," and bolted off towards my room.

When father had left us and it seemed like he wasn't coming back, I'd packed all of his things away in a trunk, letting Em use his room if she wanted. I knew it was hard for her to share a room with Lila, but when Lila had her nightmares, it was Emily who could hear her whimpering across the hall and would sleep in the bed with her until she fell back asleep.

I kneeled in front of his trunk now, searching through to the bottom for the clothes that had fit him when mother was still alive and he'd been eating more and drinking less. I held up a thick green tunic and dark brown pants, shrugging—I hoped they'd fit him well enough. I also grabbed the pair of muddy boots that sat beside the trunk, figuring it couldn't hurt for him to try them on at least.

When I got back to the living room, Bastian was in the same spot I'd left him in, flexing his fingers and toes, and twisting his limbs. I smiled and almost felt like laughing, though my stomach dropped again at seeing him. I didn't think I'd ever get used to him like this—so human, so...

He looked up and saw me, wonder still lingering in his gaze. Heat rushed up my neck and I held the clothes and boots out to him. Silently, he grabbed them from my outstretched hands, but didn't make a move to put them on. I realized then that I probably shouldn't watch him while he changed. I turned away, staring intently at the silver kettle sitting silently on the stove, hearing a faint rustling behind me.

"Alright," he said finally.

I turned back around and bit my lip to keep from smiling: the pants fit him surprisingly well, but the tunic was a bit tight across his chest.

He looked down at himself. "I feel ridiculous."

I took the couple of steps I needed to stand in front of him, where I could feel the comfort of the heat coming from him. "You look fine," I told him, standing on my toes a bit to fix his collar so that it didn't stand up. I felt him watching me, and heat rose to my cheeks again as I avoided his gaze. I wondered if he'd stared at me like this when he'd been hidden beneath his hood at the castle.

I looked down at his bare feet. "Do the boots not fit?" I asked, meeting his eyes again.

He didn't answer at first, his gaze moving over my face as if he wanted to memorize it.

I let out a trembling breath. "I'll take that as a no."

He shook his head, as if to dispel his wandering thoughts, and replied, "Not even close, but don't worry. I'm used to being barefoot."

"Maybe as the Beast," I reasoned, "but not as a human."

He grinned. "I think I can manage."

I rolled my eyes. "Men."

I caught the beginnings of a grin before he swept me into his arms and pressed his lips to mine. It was only for a moment, but it was soft and beautiful and I wanted to pull him back to me the moment it ended.

Most of our bodies still touching, I let out a shaky breath.

"Why did you do that?" I asked.

Bastian's gaze drifted to my lips, grinning. "Because I could."

*Oh.*

"Come on," I said unsteadily, grabbing his hand. "Let's go find my sisters."

# CHAPTER 28

## His Gentleness and Kindness

BASTIAN

ELLE LOOKED like she was ready to murder someone. Hair wild from the storm, she took my hand, and a current traveled between us.

I looked at her—really looked at her—since coming back from the dead and turning human again. Her jaw squared, I realized how strong she was, and I imagined there were few things that would affect her like this. But, no matter what, I wouldn't leave her side until her sisters were safe.

Her hand in mine, I wrenched open her front door, sudden rage at the men that had taken her sisters growing inside me. And for that evil lawman, Thomas, for suggesting the idea in the first place. Not to mention he'd tried to kill me. And had nearly succeeded.

Glancing up at the open sky, I saw that the storm had let up, though the clouds still hung ominously above us. Stumbling a little on the unevenness of the wet ground, I righted myself quickly, Belle's hand anchoring me. I wasn't sure how far to push this body yet since it felt so new to me, but that wasn't important. I would keep running and fighting until I couldn't anymore.

I let her lead in the charged silence. These streets were so foreign to me, and we weren't even into the main part of town yet. The cobblestone that had replaced the mud and dirt outside her home was uneven beneath my bare feet, but focusing on the way Belle's hand felt in mine, her skin against my human skin, distracted me well enough.

It took longer than I thought, hurrying past a few other cottages and farms of varying sizes, but the town was finally within our sights. It looked strange to me, and so different from the last time I'd seen it as a boy, when I'd visited with my father. We passed little French houses crammed between pristine store fronts, and I couldn't believe how much the Regime had changed Briar in my absence.

As we got closer, what I thought might've been the sounds of the city were growing louder and angrier, and we started to run.

"Oh no," was all I heard Belle say as she picked up her pace.

The noises became louder; people yelling, screaming obscenities against the Regime, their words tumbling over each other in rage.

Turning a corner, Belle stopped in her tracks, dropping my hand. We'd come to a square, where the crowd seemed to be turned towards a shop that's sign read 'Alinder's Bookshop', another clean-cut example of the Regime's handiwork. Outside that bookshop, an older man with glasses and white, unkempt hair had been pushed to his knees by a Regime soldier, a rifle pointed at his head.

"No!" Belle yelled, pushing her way through the crowd with such force that I knew this man was important to her. I followed quickly after until we came to where the crowd had parted around him. The ruckus we caused had made the townspeople fall silent, and then murmur to each other softly.

"Who's that with Belle?" one asked.

"Maybe he's a mercenary," another said hopefully.

"Or a Regime spy," a third mentioned venomously.

I ignored them all—they'd know who I was soon enough.

"Stop," Belle told the first soldier, but he didn't even look at her. The soldier next to him, on the other hand, took out his rifle and pointed it at Belle.

"Please don't hurt this man," she continued, undeterred, "he's done nothing wrong."

"You know better than to interrupt Regime business, Belle," the first one told her, and I realized that it was the soldier that Belle had known when I'd been fighting with Thomas. When I'd still been the Beast.

Though I could feel my anger rising, I knew there were more important things I needed to be focused on. From what I could see out of the corner of my eye, there were at least half a dozen Regime soldiers stationed around the bookshop, weapons pointed at unarmed citizens. But I didn't see Belle's sisters. I glanced around stealthily, searching for what I remembered of their faces from when I'd glimpsed them in the forest, and then again in the magic mirror...

*There!*

Circled by three more soldiers, the two girls huddled against each other, barely able to stay standing with how hard their knees were knocking together. My blood boiled, but I'd have to wait until the right opportunity.

"But why hurt Mr. Alinder?" Belle demanded, bringing my attention back to her as she gestured to the old man. "What has he done to warrant this kind of treatment from the Regime?"

The soldier—*Sean*, I remembered—sneered at her, and I saw that he'd gotten closer. My skin prickled with restless energy.

"I knew where you'd gotten that book the first time I caught you reading, Belle. Alinder is the only one in town with any knowledge of the old texts. So, naturally, when I became a Regime soldier, I had to tell them what I knew. Keeping things like that a secret from the Regime is against the law, especially for a soldier; there was no other choice." He smiled proudly.

Belle shook her head, and pleaded, "But Mr. Alinder is your friend."

I looked over at the old man, and saw that his fearful eyes now held tears in them.

"*Was* my friend," Sean corrected her. "Any enemy of the Regime is no friend of mine."

"He's not an enemy of the Regime," Belle exclaimed. "He's just trying to live his life. He hasn't hurt anyone—can't you just let him go?"

Sean shook his head. "Look at all the people here, Belle, come out to see the spectacle of our government exacting justice," he announced, speaking loud enough now for the entire square to hear him. "The Regime does not forgive a transgression, and the people of Briar need to learn that we won't yield to acts of treason, no matter how small."

I'd had just about had enough of this child. Without giving any warning, I swung my fist at him. It was obvious he'd barely noticed me the entire time he'd been talking to Belle, because he had little time to see the movement before he started to bring his rifle up. But he wasn't fast enough, and my knuckles hit him squarely in the jaw. He hit the ground with a sickening thud, knocked out cold, the rifle now loose in his grasp. A chorus of gasps erupted through the crowd, but no one made a move to stop me. Even the soldier who'd been holding the loaded barrel against Mr. Alinder's head was so stunned that his grip on it had gone slack.

"Get these people out of here," I muttered to Belle.

"I'm not leaving you," she said in response.

I shook my head. "I won't have any more of the people of Briar die because of me."

She looked at me for a moment before she turned away and left my side, knowing I was right. I vaguely heard her yell for everyone to go back to their homes and stay inside. But I was too focused on the soldiers in front of me, because I realized now that they all had rifles and I had nothing. For the first time in my life, I wished I was still the Beast.

"Fantastic," I mumbled, and lunged for the closest soldier.

# CHAPTER 29

## Apparently Dying

BELLE

I WATCHED as Bastian grabbed one of the soldiers and used him as a shield before taking his rifle, letting out a relieved breath as the last few townspeople left in the square fled at the sound of gunshots. Once I told them they'd likely be killed if they stayed, they dispersed fairly quickly, and soon, the streets were completely deserted.

Shaking, I grabbed a rifle that had dropped to the ground near me, aiming it at a random soldier and hitting him somewhere near his leg—I looked away before I could see him hit the ground. I couldn't think about how I might've just killed a person; I had to remember that they weren't people anymore. Sean had more than proved that.

I couldn't believe how quickly Sean had given up Mr. Alinder. They'd been neighbors since Sean was born, and Alinder had always treated him like family. Grabbing one of the bullets still in my pocket from earlier, I loaded it, my hands growing steadier now as I pulled the trigger and another soldier around Bastian went down, holding his leg in agony. He'd taken out a couple of his own and there were only two left. Despite not being the Beast anymore, I knew he could handle this.

I glanced over to where I'd seen my sisters before, but they weren't there. And neither was Mr. Alinder. Feeling panic rise in my throat, I looked around frantically, finally seeing that there was light in the bookstore when it had been dark moments ago. Rushing past Bastian fighting the only soldier left, I swung around and shot the man in the back of the kneecap. He went down easily, his screams filling the square. I turned back and wrenched open the door to the shop, Bastian on my heels.

Bookshelves had been toppled over, hundreds of volumes tossed to the ground: the Regime's doing. I didn't spare them a single glance.

"Emily! Lila!" I called out, but didn't hear anything.

Bastian put a hand on my shoulder. "Wait."

I was about to ask him why, when I heard the smallest of sounds—a whimper—coming from the back of the store.

We hurried towards it, but saw nothing. I looked behind the register and then beyond Alinder's desk—where my two sisters were bound and gagged, squirming against their bindings.

"Keep watch for Regime soldiers," I told Bastian while I took the gag off Lila first, and then Emily. They looked scared and dirty, but otherwise unharmed.

As soon as Emily's gag was off, she croaked, "It's a trap!"

"Should've guessed as much," I heard Bastian mutter.

Swinging around, I saw the two Regime soldiers that had been holding my sisters hostage lunge from the shadows at Bastian.

"Behind you!" I warned him, and he spun, hitting the first one hard with the butt of the Regime rifle, and then crashed his elbow into the face of the second. With them knocked out cold, he dragged them outside and slammed the door shut.

I helped the girls up and untied Emily's hands. "Untie Lila," I barked at her, and for once she did as she was told.

I went to the nearest shop window, peeking out from behind the dark wood frame and onto the square to look for Alinder. At first, I didn't see anyone there. Then came a loud knock at the door. Bastian looked at me and raised an eyebrow, asking me with his eyes if I could see who it was. I shook my head. He nodded, striding carefully to the front, backing up against the doorframe, rifle in hand, before opening the door a crack.

Now I could see who it was through the small sliver of light, and breathed out a sigh of relief. "Let him in," I told Bastian. "It's Mr. Alinder."

Bastian opened the door enough so that Alinder could fit through. As soon as he was inside, the old man collapsed to the floor, white as a sheet and shaking like a leaf. I went to his side as Bastian shut the door again, dead bolting it this time.

"What happened—did they hurt you?" I asked him, holding his hand in mine. It was ice-cold.

Alinder sputtered out a bone-shaking cough, but managed to push his glasses back up his nose and answer, "I saw them taking Emily and Lila across the square. I wasn't sure what had happened, but I knew it couldn't have been their faults. And when I realized you weren't with them, I knew something was wrong."

He took an unstable breath, and continued, "I went outside to stop them, or at least stall them. But they didn't take kindly to me interfering. Before I knew it, they'd hit me in the back of my knees and I was on the ground with the bad end of a rifle pointed at my head." His eyes glinted. "That's when I saw Sean Ager in a Regime uniform, breaking down the door of the shop and ransacking the place. You know the rest from there."

I grasped his hand tightly. "I'm sorry you got involved in all of this," I told him.

He shook his head and sat up onto his knees. "I'm sorry I didn't get involved with it from the beginning. I should've kept you and your sisters from that deadbeat father of yours the moment I met him, but I thought he'd keep himself from you girls on his own. I can't believe what he was willing to trade just to pay off his gambling debt."

I didn't know how Alinder knew about that, but it didn't even affect me anymore. I knew my father was recklessly negligent and only cared about himself. Now, it seemed that everyone else was finally figuring it out. "Do they still have him locked up?"

Alinder bowed his head, and didn't speak for a moment. My racing heart began to sink.

"I'm sorry, Belle," he told me softly. "He grew ill and those cells aren't well-insulated. I heard the Regime soldiers talking about it when they were doing rounds this morning: he died in the early morning hours from pneumonia."

I drew in a sharp breath through my nose, tears hot and aching behind my eyes; my stomach felt empty and gutted. I couldn't believe it. He might've turned into a terrible father after mother died, but he'd been good to me and my sisters before that, and he was still family.

But now...now he wasn't anymore. He was just *gone*.

Bastian put his hand gently on my back—I barely felt it. Shoving my palms against my eyes hard for a moment, I took a deep breath and stood. It was clear Emily and Lila hadn't heard what Alinder had said about father. They were still sitting, leaning against each other, simply staring blankly at a shelf of books. I knew this might be how Emily would act if she heard about father's death, but Lila would definitely be crying by now.

I'd tell them about it later, when we weren't in danger.

"Emily," I called to her, and she turned to look at me with empty eyes. "Did you hear anything from the Regime soldiers? Are any more coming for us?"

"The rest of the soldiers in Briar should be headed this way," she told me flatly. "Sean sent a messenger back about Alinder and his pre-Regime books, and told him that if they didn't hear back from him in half an hour that Alinder had been..."—she couldn't say killed, and I didn't blame her—"that they should come in full force. They'll be here soon, if they aren't already."

"How are we going to get out of here?" I mumbled to no one in particular.

"We can't leave," Bastian told me. My gaze snapped to his. "They'll just come after us; we need to end this here. Now."

"The boy's right," Alinder agreed. "The Regime needs to be shown that they don't belong here anymore. Not when our king has come back from the dead."

Bastian stared at Alinder. "You know who I am?"

Alinder laughed. "Of course I know who you are. I used to see you running along the corridors of the castle. I even supplied your parents with most of the books in the royal library."

Bastian grinned. "I knew I liked you."

Alinder smiled in return, pushing his glasses back up his nose. "It's good to see that you've become the man you were always meant to be."

I sighed, a permanent ache tightening around my heart like a vice. "I'm sorry, but we don't really have time for pleasantries right now. Alinder," I said, "didn't you tell me once that your father built a tunnel under the bookshop when the Regime first came to power?"

He nodded. "But I haven't been down to check on it in years. It may have caved in."

"We'll have to chance it," I countered impatiently. "I need you to bring Emily and Lila down there right now and take them as far away as you can from here. Where does it lead out?"

"I can't let you do that, Belle," he answered instead. "I'm going to help, if I can, but I won't abandon you."

I put a hand on his shoulder. "You've done so much already. Now, I need you to do one more thing for me and save my sisters."

He looked at me for a moment, then nodded. I sighed in relief—at least they'd be safe.

"It leads out to a hollow tree stump at the outskirts of the Black Forest," he told me in defeat. "Close to your family cottage, actually."

"Good," I nodded fervently. "Take them there and we'll come find you."

Emily must've heard the exchange, because she stood up quickly from where she'd been sitting with Lila. "No, I'm staying to fight!"

"Emily," I started, "you can't fight these men. They're skilled soldiers and clearly don't have much humanity left. They won't care that they're fighting a girl."

She stepped closer. "And you think that you and this *stranger* can take them on all by yourselves?"

*I'm not sure*, I thought. I said, "We're both trained, Em. You're not."

Emily scoffed. "You're not *trained*. All you know how to do is shoot animals with a bow and arrow." She met my gaze in anguish. "You know this isn't fair," she told me. "You know that I can help you!"

I reached out and squeezed her hand. "I need you and Lila to be safe. That's all that matters."

She looked over at Bastian. I realized that she had no idea who he was, and I doubted she was paying attention when Alinder mentioned knowing his parents. "Do you trust him?"

I looked at Bastian, whose piercing gaze was already on me. "With my life," I said to Emily.

I turned back to her as she folded her arms and huffed; she was angry with me, but she knew I was right. Despite her attitude, Emily was easily frightened, even by small woodland creatures, which she always swore were forest wolves—she wouldn't stand a chance against Regime soldiers.

I'd never had the time to teach her how to survive on her own, but this was the one time I didn't regret it.

In the distance, I heard what could only be the sound of dozens of hard footfalls against cobblestone. They were coming for us, and they were close.

"Go now," I told Alinder, pushing Emily towards him and Lila.

Alinder ushered my sisters through his office door quickly, but he turned back. "Don't do anything stupid, like getting yourselves killed," he told us before he disappeared behind the door, slamming it closed.

It was so quiet in the shop now. Then I laughed out loud once when I realized that I didn't have a weapon.

Bastian looked at me oddly, but he said nothing.

"Do you think we'll make it out of this?" I asked, sobering.

"I don't know."

He didn't sound afraid, only resolute in knowing that we might die in a couple of minutes.

Pulling me into his arms, he held me close. For a moment, I could pretend that Regime soldiers weren't coming for us, that we were back in his castle and out of harm's way. He released me quickly though, shattering the image.

"I'm sorry about your father," he told me, and the emptiness I'd felt when Alinder first told me grew in my stomach like a sickness.

Instead of answering Bastian, I asked, "Do you have a plan?"

He nodded, but I could see in his eyes that he wasn't going to let go what had happened with my father.

"Is there an attic to this place?" he asked, and I wondered why it would matter. I thought about the rifle in his hand and realized it would be a perfect vantage point if I could shoot from inside the shop. Then I remembered that there *was* an attic, but it was completely boarded up. The Regime had even taken out the window up there that had once showcased rare pre-Regime books and had put wooden slats in its place. But I wondered…

"Leave it to me."

I went into Alinder's office, scanning the area quickly to see if anyone could tell that there was a secret passageway under the antique rug and beneath the old floorboards. But I couldn't see anything different. Above me was the entrance to the attic, and I had to jump up to pull on the string attached to the ladder. It creaked with the effort and I knew that, just like the secret tunnel, Alinder hadn't been up there in years. After the last wooden rung had settled on the ground with a spray of dust, I climbed up the rickety steps quickly, hoping it wouldn't collapse beneath me before I reached the top.

Alinder had once told me that this attic had been filled with rare books, yes, but also children's toys and antique things. Now, though, there was nothing but dust and cobwebs. I hurried towards the other side, trying to tread lightly over the old beams.

It was easy to tell where they'd patched up the window—the wood was lighter, but obviously of a lower quality as parts of it had begun to rot. Kneeling, I reached through a small slat that had grown between two of the pieces, hoping I wouldn't get so many splinters in my fingers that it would keep me from shooting accurately, and pulled. A large chunk of the wood piece came out, and from behind it, soft gray light poured in. I bent down and looked through the gap I'd made. It was the perfect height for kneeling, and there was just enough space there that I could see to shoot.

Once I was settled, I realized that there was a lot of noise going on downstairs. I didn't dare leave my post to see what Bastian was doing, but I was sure it was strategic. He'd been the leader of his own army, after all.

My heart sank, though, as I looked outside again and saw the first of the Regime soldiers come into the square.

# CHAPTER 30

*Beauty, Beauty*

<u>BASTIAN</u>

**A**FTER PUSHING the largest bookcases in front of the door, blocking an entire window with one, and the bottom half of the other window by overturning another, I was ready. At first, I felt bad about knocking the books to the floor, but when I looked at the titles and realized that they were the only books the Regime had legalized, I felt the urge to burn them there too.

Steeling my resolve, I readied for battle. I could already see how this would play out: with the way I'd designed it, there was no way they could break through the front door without some serious weaponry. Then their only option would be the window. With them all crowding around one area, and having to take the time to step over the bookcase as well, it would be easy for Belle to pick them off one by one from her vantage point. Any that she wasn't able to take down outside would have to deal with me.

I thought about how I'd knocked out—maybe even killed—those Regime soldiers, including Sean. I hadn't given him much time to defend himself against it, but even I could see how unfeeling and callous he was. It seemed like Belle hadn't been too attached to him—which gave me a sickening sense of pride—and he hadn't even cared that the Regime he worked for had killed his own father. He'd said that he'd *deserved* it. I wondered what the Regime was doing to these men that they became this way, but that would have to wait until this was all over.

When I could be king again and take back control of Briar.

It wasn't long before I could see the first of the soldiers enter the square. They marched to the same silent beat, dressed in all back. I glimpsed something red on each of their necks and wondered what it was.

Then, as if by design, they all froze.

"Bastian!" I heard a voice that sounded eerily like Sophie's call through the front door.

"Soph?" I called back, shocked, removing the dead bolt so that she could come through.

It *was* her. Her gray hair was unusually askew and her uniform was covered in mud, but her eyes were wide and bright.

Without giving her any warning, I gripped Sophie in a gentle bear hug the moment she'd made it inside and the door was secure again—she was crying. "I can't believe it finally happened. I can't believe you're *human* again!"

"It's good to see you, Soph, but," I continued, "you shouldn't be here.

It's too dangerous. I told you to stay at the castle."

She put her hands on her hips. "And when have I ever done what you've told me?"

I shook my head at her stubbornness, about to ask her how she'd even known where to find us, when I heard heavy footsteps above me, and dust floated down from the rafters. The door of Alinder's office creaked open, and I turned to find Belle standing in the doorway.

"Did you see what's happened to the soldiers? They just—"

But then she saw Sophie.

"Sophie?" she managed, looking as if she'd seen a ghost.

I peered outside again, and saw that the soldiers hadn't moved. I tensed, feeling in my bones that Sophie being here wasn't just happenstance.

"Sophie," I started. "What's going on?"

But when I turned back to her, she simply smiled at me. And then she started to glow.

# CHAPTER 31

## *He Still Breathed*

<u>BELLE</u>

THE MOMENT I'd seen Sophie, I knew something wasn't right. She smiled sadly at Bastian when he asked her what was going on, and then a light began to grow from her chest, starting low like the ember of a fire, and burning white-hot until it had lit up the entire bookshop. Bastian tried to reach for her, but I pulled him back. Something told me that he shouldn't get involved—that this was important.

Sophie became too bright to look at as the light consumed her, and I had the strangest feeling that I'd seen this before, but couldn't remember when.

When the light finally extinguished, a beautiful woman had taken Sophie's place.

Before I had a chance to take in her appearance, though, she was right in front of me, reaching out to touch my face.

"Remember, child," she whispered, and her hand brushed my forehead. Intense heat emanated from her palm and it felt like it was burning me. Then…

I remembered the dream.

The first night I'd been at the castle, this same woman had come to me in a dream, saying she knew my mother and that she was proud of me for sacrificing my life for my family's. I also remembered her telling me that she was one of the fair folk, and that I'd be rewarded for what I'd done.

But the thing I remembered most from the dream became clear in my mind: *"Only when Bastian has a firm grasp on his kingdom again will what I've told you today be remembered."*

As quickly as it had come, her hand left my forehead and I felt myself falling backwards. I waited for my head to crack against the stone of the shop floor, but someone caught me. I opened my eyes to see that it was Bastian, but he wasn't looking at me. He was glaring at the fairy with loathing and hatred. He pulled me to him, holding me tight, and I reveled for a moment in the feeling of safeness that enveloped me.

"What did you do with Sophie, you bitch?" he demanded, and I was so surprised by his words that I stepped back from him.

Shaking my head, I started to explain, "Bastian—"

"It's alright, Belle," the fairy said, and I looked back to her. She looked exactly the same as she had in my dream. "He only knows me as the witch who cursed him and nothing more." She turned her gaze to Bastian. "I'll try to explain, if you'll allow it."

I looked at Bastian with pleading eyes, and though I could see the anger in his gaze and in the way that he held himself as if he were ready to attack her at any moment, he nodded.

She clapped her hands. "Good! I'll start from the beginning then."

I shook my head. "We don't have time for this. The soldiers—"

She waved her hand dismissively. "I'll show you what needs to be shown and nothing more. No time will pass in the mortal realm."

With a flick of her wrist, the fallen bookshelves and faded brick walls of the shop melted away, leaving in its wake a softened, almost dream-like, state of the outside of the castle, one without the Black Forest surrounding it.

A figure walked towards the iron gate. They turned for a second and I gasped: it was a younger version of Sophie. There were so few wrinkles on her face that I almost didn't recognize her, but her eyes remained just as bright as they were now.

"The fairy council came to an agreement the year Bastian was born," I heard Sophie say, even though I couldn't see her. "Something had to be done about the Regime. The king of Briar was one of the few leaders of the world left who'd abstained from giving in to the corrupt usurpers, and that made the Emperor want his crown all the more. I was sent to the castle in the guise of a governess for his newborn son in order to maintain that ideal. For if the Emperor took Briar, a place where the fair folk had escaped to from so many parts of the world, we would cease to exist and Briar would fall not long after."

I found Bastian's hand and took it without looking at him. He didn't seem to notice as the scene changed to a younger Bastian in his bedchambers, yelling something unintelligible at Sophie.

"My many years as your governess, Bastian, made me realize that, in your arrogant state, you couldn't possibly uphold your father's resolve. When he died, you became impossible, tyrannical, and vain to your very core."

My hand tightened around his.

The scene shifted again, this time to Bastian looking at himself in a floor-length mirror, dressed in flashy military garb, like I'd seen in the rose-tea visions. This wasn't the Bastian I knew. This Bastian was cold and calculating, each movement purposeful and filled with pride and vanity. His gaze was hard and unyielding. This looked like a man who wanted to burn down the world.

"The fey elders reconvened and it was decided that something needed to be done about *you*. Removing you from the throne would guarantee the destruction of Briar with most certainty, so we had to work with what we had."

Now Bastian's hand tightened around mine at her words.

"That was when I cursed you," she continued, sounding saddened by it. The scene changed once more, playing out Bastian's interaction with the old woman, who he took the ring from greedily and shut out in the cold.

"I knew you would spurn the affections of an old, ugly woman, and take the ring, believing it would give you the power you sought. After you were cursed to become the Beast, I also knew that you'd keep Sophie— well, me—around. I'd been like a mother to you, and loved you even when you'd been terrible to me. The fey council agreed that the curse would give you humility and grace and would teach you to earn another's love rather than expecting and demanding it. They said it would help you grow up into the king you *could* be." She sighed, and a new scene appeared with Bastian sitting alone in the greenhouse as the Beast, his eyes dead as they peered sightless out of the darkened emerald windows. "But I could see what it was doing to you. It tore you apart from the inside, and there was nothing I could do about it. There are very few things a fairy can do to change a curse once it's been cast, and you needed to see it through to the end."

Then, the images of the past disappeared, and the bookshelves came back into view. The fairy stood before us, barely floating above the dusty floorboards as she spoke to me. "I'd almost lost hope before you came, Belle. But once I'd seen you—seen the loyalty and fierceness and kindness in your heart—I knew you were the one that would break the curse."

She looked at us both solemnly. "I wish I could've told you, but you had to find out on your own." Then she spoke only to Bastian. "I know it seems like I betrayed you, but my concern for you has always been genuine. When I became your governess, a part of me became human. I knew the curse needed to be fulfilled, but I stayed after the deed was done because I couldn't stand the thought of you trying to break it on your own." She bowed her head. "Still, I never told you who I was and my role in your curse, and for that I am truly sorry."

I turned to Bastian, my eyes searching his, pleading with him to forgive her. Yes, she'd tricked him. But, if I remembered correctly from my reading of them, that was the way of the fey. They were cruel to a fault, believing humans to be weak creatures. And I was sure she'd changed, just as she'd said.

Bastian finally looked at me and he seemed a bit defeated. He sighed before turning back to her.

"I'll forgive you on one condition," he told her, and she perked up. "You tell me your name—your *real* name."

The hope slipped from her face and she swallowed hard, crestfallen. "That's the one thing I cannot give out on a whim, Bastian. In the Otherworld, if someone were to know my true name, they could make me do anything they wanted. *Anything.*"

"We're not in the Otherworld, fairy," he told her, and there was still venom left in his words. "I understand why you did what you did. I'm a better man for it, and it allowed me to meet Belle. But you took my name from me for five years, knowing I would call myself the Beast. So I think it's only fair that I know your true name."

The fairy smiled slightly. "You've been in my company for far too long. My stubbornness and cunning has rubbed off on you."

Without waiting for an answer, she began to shrink, growing smaller and smaller until she was the size of a thimble, hovering in the air. I'd always expected fairies to have wings, but I didn't see any on her.

She zoomed toward us, coming between our ears and speaking in a whisper, "You must promise not to tell a single soul my true name, and promise never to call me by that name. For even though we're not in the Otherworld, knowing the name of a fair folk will still allow you some hold over them."

I nodded in understanding, though Bastian didn't move a single muscle, and together we leaned in closer as she said, "My name is Eglantina. It means wild rose."

I felt myself smiling at that.

"In a moment," she continued, though she was no longer whispering, "my hold on the soldiers outside will weaken and disappear. Your sisters and your Mr. Alinder are safe for the moment, but I'm giving you the chance to escape. Remain brave, my young humans. The hard times are not over yet."

I looked over at Bastian, my questioning gaze meeting his wary one. Then we both looked up at the fairy, who was back to her normal, human size now. Smiling at us again, she lifted her fingers, snapped them, and disappeared in a flash of purple smoke.

# CHAPTER 32

*Yes, Dear Beast*

BASTIAN

AND SHE was gone.

There was an overwhelming rushing sound in my head, like the relentless wind in a heavy storm. An anger I'd never felt before had begun to consume me, starting in my heart and spreading to my entire body.

Belle squeezed my hand, grounding me, and I realized that I was shaking.

"Bastian," she said softly. "Bastian, look at me."

I did. My hand still in hers, she stood in front of me now. Her deep brown eyes pleaded with me, forcing me to truly look at her. Her face was marked with dirt, her hair wild, lips chapped; there were red marks around her neck from when Thomas had choked her. A wave of protectiveness washed over me, dulling the anger.

"I know this hurts. I know it's unfair and feels like the worst kind of betrayal." She touched my cheek with her other hand gently, and I felt myself leaning into her. I thought about the moment we'd had in the castle library, of her touching my face for the first time, and some of the weight lifted off my chest. "But we don't have the luxury of being angry right now. We need to move quickly, before the soldiers reanimate."

"You're right," I told her. "I just can't believe..."

"I know," she said again. "But we have to go."

I nodded, following her towards the back of the shop as my resolve hardened. Once we were in Alinder's office, I shut the door and locked it.

"Open the hatch," she started, "just beneath that rug there."

Kneeling, I flipped over the corner of the rug nearest me and kept moving it back until I found a handle that blended almost perfectly into the floorboards. When I looked back up, Belle was rifling through one of the shelves.

"What are you looking for?" I asked, standing.

"Just a couple books," she answered without turning, "a Book of Fairytales and Alinder's copy of Hamlet."

*Of course*, I thought, shaking my head but unable to stop myself from falling in love with her a little more in that moment.

"Ah, there you are," she mumbled to herself.

When she turned back around, books in hand, I was grinning.

"What?" she asked.

"Nothing," I chuckled.

She gave me a look before hopping down into the passageway. I climbed in after her, reaching around the top of the hatch for the rug to pull over it and closing it softly.

Darkness enveloped us, until Belle lit a match and grabbed one of the torches pinned to wall beside us. She peered back at me silently, brow drawn together.

"What's wrong?" I asked, taking her hand.

"Everything will be different once we come out on the other side of this tunnel."

"It's already different, Belle," I said, pulling her towards me slightly. "Everything changed that night you entered the Black Forest. But this change will be good, I promise."

She nodded, not looking very convinced, and we started towards her family's cottage.

~

I squinted against the harsh sunlight when we finally reached the end of the passageway and crawled out through the dead trunk of a forest tree.

Belle had been quiet the entire way, and I hadn't wanted to interrupt her silence, even though it was driving me mad not knowing what she was thinking. I was sure there was just as much going on in her head as there was in mine.

I wasn't sure where we were until she started running and I finally saw it: Belle's cottage. I didn't have the best memories of it, but it was her home—and that was enough to push aside any feelings I had towards it.

Belle started pulling away from me, and I noticed that I was completely out of breath. I didn't understand it at first.

*You've had a long day, turning back into a human, fighting off Regime soldiers*, I thought, but something didn't quite feel right.

Belle looked back at me and slowed when she saw that I wasn't keeping up. I waved her on—her sisters were much more important. She gave me a small smile and then hurried on. I watched her fling the door open, heard shouts of happiness as black dots flashed across my vision. My stomach roiled. *What's wrong with me?*

Without warning, my knees buckled beneath me and I crashed to the muddied winter ground. I tried to move my arms, my legs—but nothing worked.

"Belle," I managed, but it sounded like less than a whisper. My eyes closed, and I could swear that I heard her calling my name.

Then I lost consciousness.

# CHAPTER 33

## All Made of Fireflies

<u>BELLE</u>

I HELD my sisters tightly in my arms. I never thought I'd get to see them again, but here they were. And I was never letting them out of my sight.

"Did you run into any trouble?" I asked, pulling back only a fraction. I stroked Lila's fine hair, still not believing that they were here. That we were all safe, at least for the moment.

"None at all," Alinder said, and I looked up at him. He was smiling. I wanted to reach out and hug him too, but that would mean letting go of my sisters, and I wasn't ready to do that just yet. It was hard to believe that we had all escaped the Regime soldiers, alive. It was almost too good to be true.

"Where's Bastian?" Alinder asked.

I turned towards the empty doorway, a strange feeling in the pit of my stomach. "He was right behind me."

Leaving the reaching arms of Emily and Lila was almost like tearing skin from bone, but something wasn't right.

Peering out the front door into the rare sunlight of winter, I searched the trees for him, not seeing—then I caught something on the ground.

It was Bastian.

I'd started to run towards him without realizing it. "Bastian!" I screamed, but he didn't move.

*No, no, not again. Not after all we've been through.*

I knelt beside him, my hand on his back. I could feel the shallow movement that meant he was still breathing, but barely. Panicked and desperate, I did the only thing I could think of.

"Eglantina," I whispered.

The name was met with silence. I opened my mouth to yell it, but found I had no air in my lungs to expel it. The fairy materialized in front of me then, looking like she wouldn't mind murdering me.

"How dare you summon me with my true name?" she demanded.

"I'm sorry, but Bastian," I looked back down at him, able to breathe easily once again. "He's hurt."

I heard the fairy take in a shallow breath. "I thought this might happen."

My gaze shot back to her. "That *what* might happen?"

"He became too dependent on the magic that the curse gave him," she explained, shaking her head.

"Are you saying there's nothing you can do?"

"That's not what I said," she snapped, then sighed. "There's only one thing that might save him. But you'll have to get him to the castle."

"Me?" I gawked. "Can't you use your magic to send us there yourself?"

She laughed. "I'm already in trouble with the council for how much I've meddled in this. No," she continued, "this you will have to do on your own."

I stared at her. *Some magic fairy you are.* "Can you at least give me a horse?"

"I cannot conjure objects out of thin air," she said, then looked thoughtful. "But I can call one to you."

At that, she disappeared.

"Wait!" I called out, but she was gone.

I reached underneath Bastian, turning him over with some effort so that I could get a better look at him. One side of his face was red and covered in mud, and his eyes were closed. I cupped his cheek, my fingers touching the silver scars at his neck.

"Hold on, Bastian" I told him. "I'll never forgive you if you die on me now."

Part of me hoped to see him grin at that, but he remained as he was.

Then, I heard the galloping of hooves. *What the——?*

Bastian's brown mare burst into the clearing, neighing and huffing as it came to stand next to us. I'd never been so happy to see a horse; I thought it'd been lost to us for good. Immediately, it kneeled down, and I could only assume that it was waiting for me to put Bastian on its back. But even in this human form, he'd be too heavy for me to lift.

"Em, Alinder: come quickly!" I called out.

They rushed out of the cottage, Lila trailing them curiously.

"Hurry, help me get him on the horse," I said, grabbing an arm. Em grabbed the other arm, Alinder grabbed his legs, and the three of us managed to drape him over the beast.

"What happened?" Em breathed out once I'd mounted the horse behind him.

I shook my head. "I'm not sure, but I can't let him die."

Turning to Alinder, I said. "Take my sisters back into the mouth of the tunnel. With Bastian and I gone, I can't guarantee everyone's safety, and the Regime may come for you."

Alinder nodded assuredly past the fear in his eyes.

I turned the horse towards the Black Forest, and took off, riding as fast as I dared.

# CHAPTER 34

## The Terrible Enchantment

BASTIAN

WHEN I opened my eyes, the world around me was spinning. I thought I could make out the stone walls of my castle, spattered with brown and blue color. *It can't be...*

But when I focused on the face in front of me, I saw Belle, and the world settled.

"Bastian?" she asked, hopeful.

I grinned at her, though I'm not sure my lips quite moved that way. A single tear escaped down her cheek as she threw her arms around me. I went to put my arms around her in return, but then she sat up again and slapped me on the arm.

"What was that for?" I groaned, my voice grating against my throat like it was made of sandpaper.

"For almost dying again," she told me as her cheeks turned pink.

I reached for her, but winced at the pain in my side. Concern colored her features, and her eyes searched my face, my neck, my chest. Then she stopped at my side, where I'd been bleeding since the beginning of the fight with the Regime soldiers. It had stung only a little up until now, but it didn't take long for it to feel like I was being bitten there by hundreds of red fire ants.

"You're hurt," she murmured, reaching for the tear in my shirt, and she started to pull and rip at it.

I watched her work at the threads to get to the wound, and was struck again by her beauty. Not just the obviousness of her, but the way her cheeks flushed when she looked at me, her overwhelming need to protect her sisters, the way her eyes would grow fierce when she told me she loved me. As if I needed to be convinced of it when it had saved my life.

After trying to tear at the fabric with little success, she looked up to see that I was grinning at her. "This would be a lot easier if I didn't have a shirt on," I told her. "All you need to do is ask."

She shot me a look, but I could see that she was trying not to smile.

Chuckling, I tried to pull my shirt over my head, but the pain at my side screamed that that wasn't an option. Instead, I undid the buttons before tossing it to the floor, hearing a quiet gasp escape her lips once it was gone. Her gaze strayed to the parts of me that had been hidden under all the fur, until finally landing on the wound again.

"It doesn't look too bad," Belle told me as she touched the skin around it gently. "I don't see any broken bones, and the gash is more like a deep scratch." She grabbed up the shirt and tore it apart further, making strips out of it before tying one around my entire torso that was just thick enough to cover the gash. I hissed in pain when she placed the cloth over it, and she smiled apologetically without meeting my gaze.

When she was done, we sat there for a moment, not quite looking at each other. God, I wanted to touch her—I wanted to touch her so badly it was physically painful. Now that we weren't in immediate danger, there were so many things I wanted to...

She seemed to have a sudden thought, because she finally looked at me and asked, "You don't have your magic anymore, do you?"

I shook my head, strangely disappointed. "I know that the only reason I had the magic in the first place was because of the curse. And now that I'm not cursed anymore, it makes sense that it's gone." I looked down at my hands. "But it still feels so strange. I almost miss it."

But losing my magic made me think about the witch that had cursed me, about Sophie.

*Sophie.*

I still couldn't believe that, all that time, the witch had been right under my nose, impersonating someone I loved. I'd forgiven the fairy for Belle's sake, but I wasn't sure I was really ready to yet. I knew having the fairy's real name would come in handy one day; I might've been a changed man, but I wasn't stupid.

"What happened?" I asked Belle.

Belle's voice trembled when she answered, "Sophie said that you'd become too dependent on the magic and—"

"Sophie?" I cut her off.

She looked surprised. "Oh," she breathed out. "I'm sorry Bastian, I had no other choice. For all I knew, you were dying, and so I called her by her real name and she told me how to make you better."

"And you trusted her!" I roared, an unchecked anger rising in me.

Belle sat up straighter. "I didn't have any other choice; I wasn't going to let you die."

Huffing, I tried to calm down. *You'd have done the same thing for her, no matter how much you hate Sophie*, I told myself. I sighed.

"I'm sorry, you're right." I took her hand in mine, still marveling at the fact that I could touch her skin with my own. "How did you heal me?"

"It was the roses," she told me, her shoulders relaxing. "Even though you lost your magic, they still hold it within them. In the petals, the leaves, the roots. Soph—*she* said that you'll have to ingest them every day until we can ween you off. It's the only way."

I shook my head. "I hate this. Even when I think the curse is gone, it keeps coming back."

Belle didn't answer at first, but instead smiled, placing her hand on my cheek.

"We'll get through this," she said finally. "All of this, together."

I placed my hand over hers, and I believed her.

# CHAPTER 35

## Her Long-Loved Prince

BELLE

ASTIAN GAVE me a lopsided grin, and I stopped breathing for a second. Not long ago, those teeth had been sharp, jutting fangs, but now they were perfectly straight.

Trying to smile in return, my legs wobbled underneath me from exhaustion and I moved to sit fully on the bed, Bastian still holding my hands. The last few days were finally catching up to me, and while I felt like I could sleep for the next week, I also thought that if I closed my eyes, I'd wake up and all of this would have been a dream.

Soon, we'd have to head back towards the cottage to bring my sisters and Alinder to the safety of the castle. But, for now, it was all I could do to keep my eyes from closing.

Bastian dropped my hands, threading them through his hair and staring down at himself, a small smile on his lips, and I suddenly felt cold.

I looked at him again—*really* looked at him. He was handsome and so different now, sitting an arm's length away from me. Without a shirt to cover him up, my cheeks heated, remembering our kiss at the cottage. I'd never done something like that before: being bold enough to take what I wanted. Now, I couldn't help wondering if he felt the same way.

I folded my hands in my lap and stared at them. I felt foolish even thinking it, but if I'd known that he looked like this underneath his curse, I would've never believed that he could love me. I'd told him my scars didn't define me, but they hadn't mattered so much until now. I was much more vain than I'd believed I could be, but some part of me thought I wasn't deserving of his love. The only people in my life who had truly loved were my sisters and my mother, who had to love me unconditionally because we were blood.

Bastian had no such obligation.

The sheets shifted as he moved close to me again, but I didn't look up.

"Belle?" he asked. "What's wrong?"

"Nothing," I replied as I wiped away a traitorous tear, my palm still caked in dried blood.

"I've been a Beast for the past five years," he said, "and still I can tell that you're keeping something from me."

I managed a small breath of a laugh, reaching towards him without taking my eyes off my legs. But I dropped my hand just as quickly.

"I thought you'd like me better this way," he said with an odd lilt to his voice.

That made me look up at him. Impossible sadness filled his gaze.

"It never mattered to me what you looked like, Bastian," I promised him, confused. "I loved you even when you were the Beast. You're kind and smart and a good man."

He placed a hand over mine and a tinge of warmth flooded me. "Then what is it?"

In answer, I pulled my hand from his to touch my cheek, tracing the indents of the silver scars there, and the ones on my neck, avoiding the fresh wound made by Thomas. My fingers shook as more tears spilled, unwarranted, and I tried to compose myself.

"All I can think about," I started, "is that you'll see yourself as you were before and won't...*want* me anymore."

He was quiet for a moment, before he was suddenly very close to me, his nearness undoing any sense I had left. He touched my scars gently and I shivered.

"Your scars make you more beautiful to me," he said, and I bit my lip. "They're a part of who you are. And I love you, Belle. Every part of you." He turned my head gently so that I had look at him. His blue eyes pierced mine. "Nothing will ever change that."

A shuddering breath left me at his words. Without thinking, I reached for him and my lips crushed against his, knocking us backwards onto the bed. His lips were frozen in surprise for a moment before they grew soft and supple, moving against mine like we'd done this a thousand times, his arms encasing my body.

*Oh,* I sighed, my lungs feeling like the breath had been stolen from them.

It took me a moment to realize that I was on top of Bastian on his bed, but I was too lost in him to care.

Holding me close, he spun us so that I was under him. His lips separated from my mouth, gently kissing every inch of my scarred cheek with a tender, scorching heat, before moving to my neck, the feel of him consuming me. I made a small whimpering sound when his lips brushed my collarbone and his hands swept along the bare skin just above my waist, where my tunic had ridden up.

His lips captured mine again, one of his hands slowly, softly moving up towards my rib cage where the scars continued. My back arched up against him involuntarily, and I could hear his breathing hitch—his hands were shaking slightly when he cupped my cheek. He flicked his tongue against my lips and I opened my mouth to him, his tongue sweeping tenderly to meet mine.

He groaned against my lips when my hands caressed down his back, feeling the indents of his own scars there. I touched the skin above his pants, before I slipped my fingertips just beneath the band and dug into his skin. His other hand, which was still under my shirt, went to the middle of my bare back, holding me there, pressing me to him so that my chest brushed against his—and I gasped in pain.

He eased off of me quickly, kneeling on the bed. "Did I hurt you?"

I didn't answer as an ache I couldn't place shot all along my body, coming from my chest. I sat up and turned away from him. "I think it might just be a bruise," I said quietly. I pulled down the front collar of my tunic to see what had stung so badly...

"What the hell," I managed. Carved in red and black ink, on the skin just above my heart, was a briar rose in bloom, the black thorny stem reaching from where the petals sat over my heart, curling down between my breasts where it stopped.

"Have you always had that?" Bastian asked curiously.

"No," I told him, completely bewildered. Who could've done this? Sophie maybe?

He was silent for a moment. "Actually, I like it."

I rolled my eyes.

"How…" he began, looking thoughtful until anger marred his face.

"This is the witch's work," Bastian said through his teeth, and I instinctively wrapped my arms around his waist, hoping to diffuse his anger.

"It's not that bad. Really," I said. And it wasn't. In fact, it almost made sense. Maybe it was to remind Bastian of who'd broken the curse for him, and to remind me of the same. Maybe it was to remind us both that black magic always left a mark. "You said you like it?"

A deep longing lingered in his gaze when he looked back at me. "Oh yes."

I played with the hairs at the back of his neck. "Then it can't be that bad."

He smiled, bringing his lips down on mine. I brought my hands from where they'd been attached to his waist to trace up his back, pressing him to me again—and he growled, breaking off the kiss.

"What's wrong?" I asked. But something I hadn't noticed before on Bastian caught my eye, and I saw that he had a mark over his heart as well, the black ink sitting on top of the silver scars there. It was in the same place as mine, but instead of a rose, it was an intricate design of a wolf howling, with black swirls and dots lining the inside of the creature's shape.

I laughed. "At least she has a sense of humor."

When Bastian didn't answer, I looked up to see that he was seething. "Hasn't she done enough to me?"

I touched his face, and his features barely softened. "If it's any consolation, I like yours."

After a moment, he shook his head and chuckled, and I looked into his eyes as he cupped my face. The anger left his gaze almost as soon as it had come.

"This—being able to touch you the way I want to—it will never get old," he told me, his thumb brushing against my lips. My heart thundered wonderfully in my chest

Staring at me for a moment longer, he spoke again, "I have something I need to tell you."

All I could do was nod as he stood from the bed and went over to the armoire. "Let me put a shirt on first."

"That's not really necessary," I said, and he snorted a laugh as he pulled a long-sleeve tunic from an open drawer and dropped it over his head. It was creased and wrinkled; I imagined this was the first time he'd taken it out in five years. But it didn't matter. Bastian would look good in a grain sack.

"Nevertheless," he said, his entire body shuddering, "it's probably a good idea."

"Cold?" I wondered, trying to hide a grin.

His hand cupped the back of his neck awkwardly. "It's strange:

without my fur, I find I'm freezing all the time now."

"You'll just have to learn to live without fur like the rest of us."

He chuckled, and I was growing used to the lightness of his voice now that he was no longer the Beast. "It was a hard thing to imagine not long ago."

Stepping towards me, he took my hand in his. "Belle, I…" he laughed softly. "I used to be so much better at this."

"Bastian…" I breathed his name, not thinking of anything else to say.

He took a deep breath before he spoke again, but I felt like I could barely breathe at all.

"From the moment I first saw you in the Black Forest, hunting pheasants and deer for you and your sisters, I wanted to know you better."

"Wait," I said, trying to wrap my head around his words, "you were watching me?"

Bastian's cheeks heated, and he ran his fingers through his hair as he replied, "Yes."

I fought back a smile because, while I felt sort of violated from not knowing he'd been watching me, it didn't stop me from loving him. "I'll pretend you didn't say that."

He turned serious, but hope lingered in his gaze. "I don't expect anything from you, Belle. My life won't be easy after today now that I have a kingdom to rule, and I'd be a fool to think you'd consider being with me after all I've put you through."

Pausing, Bastian went to his knees beside the bed, and I leaned towards him. "But I promise you that I'll always be by your side and love you every day of my life, if you'll allow me to, as my father did for my mother."

I couldn't help smiling, as if the expression were permanent. He was so unsure of himself and my feelings for him, just as I had been about his feelings for me. He'd more than proved that he loved me, and I'd do everything I could to convince him that I'd never loved anyone more than I loved him.

I kneeled on the floor beside him, placing both hands on his chest and tipping my head up to place a lingering kiss on his lips.

"You have my heart, Bastian," I said simply. "It's never belonged to anyone else, and it never will."

He closed his eyes, and I wondered if he was thinking about what it would be like for me to be here all the time with him. And when he opened his eyes again, I had hope that he liked that idea very much.

"Let's go get your sisters and Alinder."

# EPILOGUE

## *With the Utmost Splendor*

### BELLE

A WEEK later, we had father's funeral.

Upon hearing of Thomas' death, the Regime soldiers in Briar were called back by the Emperor, and we hadn't seen another black uniform in the village since. And as no one was there to enforce Regime laws, they no longer had a hold over the town. It didn't take long for people to recall what it had been like before the Regime had taken over our quiet town; they remembered the things they'd once enjoyed doing that they hadn't been able to for so long. You could see it in the way everyone greeted each other, that there was a weight lifted off our shoulders.

They also remembered Bastian, their king, not that his curse had been lifted.

That day, we'd found Alinder and my sisters hidden in the entrance to the passageway, completely unharmed, if not a little dirty. And we didn't need a horse this time to lead them back to castle, where they would be safe. Apparently, when the Beast's curse had been lifted, the forest wolves had disappeared, allowing us safe passage. The trees, too, had lost their thorns and their darkness. I wondered how much those things had been a very real manifestation of Bastian's fears, taking the shape of the dark magic he'd come to possess.

Thomas' death, though, haunted me too. I'd done what I had to do, and I hadn't purposefully tried to kill him. But he was dead now because of me, and I was trying to live with myself, no matter the kind of person he'd been.

Helping Bastian was distraction enough. He hadn't had much time after that day to think about what the next steps were. Before the dust could settle and the town fell to lawless chaos, he'd had to establish his authority as the king. He'd done the best of it he could, but we knew it would take some time before the people of Briar felt like they could trust him again.

Now, one of his arms was curled tightly around my shoulders and I was leaning into him as they burned my father's lifeless body on a pyre. It was the funeral that he'd asked for in his will, and I abided by his wishes. The guilt I felt for not checking in on him earlier weighed on me. It was hard not to blame myself for his death too, even though he'd been the one to create this whole mess in the first place. There were a lot of things I'd done wrong lately, but I believed he was in a better place now.

And I knew I couldn't be too hard on him since his mistakes had brought me to Bastian.

As he pressed his lips into my hair, I bit the inside of my mouth to keep the tears away. Lila, who was sitting cross-legged on the grass, had finally stopped bawling and now was only hiccupping every once in a while, and Emily looked like she still wasn't coming close to crying. Even when I'd told them about it, my younger sister had just stood there as if I'd been telling her about the weather. Em was too jaded for only being thirteen, but she'd lived a hard enough life to warrant it. We all had.

After I couldn't look at the burning flames anymore, I left Bastian's embrace and pulled Lila up into my arms.

"Come on, sweet girl," I said as her legs wrapped around my torso. "We're going home."

"Where's home?" she mumbled into my shoulder, and my heart broke a little more.

"Our new home, of course," I told her, and my eyes found Bastian's. He was looking at me, his gaze intense as he watched me with my sister.

"With him?" She pointed to Bastian.

Bastian and I hadn't had the chance to talk much about. He'd said it was already decided that my sisters and I—and Alinder too—were moving into the castle permanently. He made it clear that I didn't owe him anything for it, that we deserved to be happy. But I'd told him exactly what I'd said to him before: that he had my heart. I already loved him more than I thought I ever could love another person, and even though it scared me to think too far ahead, it felt right.

I smiled at her. "Yes, Lila—in a castle."

"A castle!" she squealed and I laughed as she scrambled out of my arms, running straight towards Bastian.

He peered down at her with a strange expression and I held back another laugh. I could tell by the look on his face that he'd never dealt with children. I'm sure he thought she was some bizarre creature he'd never encountered before and definitely didn't trust.

"She's harmless," I called out to him, and he shot me a panicked look.

Lila reached for his hand, grabbing at his finger, and he let her. I felt Em come up next to me and I locked our hands together.

"Ready?" I asked, looking past Bastian and into what had been the Black Forest. Even now, the darkness of the trees continued to change from burnt black to dark brown and emerald green, and I no longer felt frightened by it.

"Not really," she admitted.

I squeezed her hand. "We'll be fine, Em. I promise."

She didn't say anything, and I wasn't sure she was convinced. I knew Bastian would take care of us, and it would be good for him not to be alone in the castle. I could see us having a life there; a good life.

There was so much we were still unsure about, though, and I knew that that's where Em's thoughts were: if the people of Briar would fully accept Bastian as their king; how long Briar would be able to evade the reaching claws of the Regime; if we could find a way to move on and rebuild; if we would ever see Sophie—or any of the fair folk—again.

I walked over with Emily's hand still in mine to where Bastian was holding Lila in his arms. Her head was placed perfectly in the crook of his neck and it seemed that she'd fallen asleep. He still looked awkward holding her, but it was sweet.

Seeing us all together, I realized that none of those other things mattered now. We could survive anything, as long as we had love.

# ACKNOWLEDGEMENTS

I'm not sure where to begin with these acknowledgements. I have no agent to thank, no publisher or professional editor to praise. But I have something better: a wonderful husband who has supported my writing since we meet over 11 years ago. And I have my parents, who were proud that I knew what I wanted to be when I grew up, even if that was being a writer.

This book is a true labor of love. It was never my intention to have this book published traditionally, and I think that's what makes it so special. This is my love letter to a story that shaped my childhood and still rings true the older I get, and if I never make a penny from this story, I'll still be happy to have shared it with the world because of how much it means to me.

I want to thank those that read early drafts of my book online and made such helpful comments. A very special thanks to Janelle Fluharty, who was willing to read this on a tight deadline. Then there's Heather Croissant, who designed the gorgeous cover and the wonderful chapter art; you brought to life what I'd dreamed up in my head, and I will be forever grateful.

I couldn't be more thankful to all the wonderful friends and family that always supported my writing: Michelle Gernert, Michelle Conklyn, my grandmother Dolly Mainardi, my parents-in-law, my cousins (especially Brian Fox, who I have a distinct memory of him telling me never to stop writing). Everyone else, you know who you are, and I love you.

Finally, I want to thank readers everywhere. It's because of you that I want my stories to be told. And I can't wait to share more of them with you!

NICOLE MAINARDI was born in San Diego, California, despite her protests otherwise. Spending her childhood in Michigan and Arizona, she finally found her roots back in Southern California, where she met her husband in their junior year of high school.

When she's not writing, she's working at her day job, reading, obsessing over Harry Potter and all things Disney, and playing soccer.

Visit nmainardi.blogspot.com for more information and news!

Made in the USA
San Bernardino, CA
27 May 2019